ROUND MIDNIGHT

The short listed stories from
Eyelands 9th
international short story contest

ROUND MIDNIGHT
Collection of short stories
Creative director: Costas Malousaris
Editor: Gregory Papadoyiannis
Cover by strangeland

strange days books

Strange Days Books
Social Cooperative Publishing House
Address: Chimarras 6, Rethymno, 74100, Crete, Greece
tel:+2831503835
email: strangedaysbooks@gmail.com
www.facebook.com/STRANGEDAYSBOOKS
Copyright© Strange Days Books
Cover design: © *strangeland*

www.eyelands.gr
e-mail: eyelandsmag@gmail.com
facebook: www.facebook.com/eyelands.portal/
contests: eyelandscontes.wordpress.com
eyelands awards: eyelandsawards.com

Strange Days in the world / EE -11
Printed in Greece by Preprint
ISBN: 9781700174369

CONTENTS

4

GRAND PRIZE
Marvin Baxter's Background Music
Javi Reddy

The first time Marvin Baxter heard Nina Simone, his mother was in another room, with a man who had no biological connection to him. The first time Marvin heard Louis Armstrong, the same man sent his mother crashing through the dining room table. By the time he'd heard Ella Fitzgerald for the first time, his mother was humming, before letting her son know that this was the man she couldn't wait to marry. As Marvin's eyes tracked the uninterrupted swaying of his mother's hips through the kitchen, he could not help but gaze upon the bruises on her arms. He gently laid down his fork and grabbed a handful of saucy spaghetti, before fiddling with it within his palm. As his mother continued to sing the praises of her new-found love, Marvin zoned out.His7 year old neurons were on a mission. Whenever life's noise became too heavy, Marvin Baxter had the background music. And he was grateful that it existed, only in his head.

Mother and son packed up their modest belongings and moved into their latest home, which Marvin soon realised was far less spacious than their former abode. Being crammed in that close, especially at the dinner table, meant he could almost stretch out his tongue to taste his mother's tears. And if he swivelled his head the other way around, he could take a whiff of what a man should smell like once he'd self-destructed and let go of any remaining personal hygiene. That was Lloyd's gift to him- being a worse father than an actual father who had abandoned him.

Marvin could not bring his vinyl player with him to the new flat, for there was no space to plug it in. Space was a curious matter in their new household. Marvin often wondered why their cupboards were so big, when there was hardly any food in them. With Lloyd's mysterious 'car tyre business' threatening to turn matters around soon, the income was less than consistent. All Marvin could do was hope his next meal would extend beyond stale crackers and ripe fruit. He'd not had spaghetti in months which mainly upset him when he could not remember what the texture felt like on his tongue, as he played with it before swallowing it.

Marvin needed his background music more and more. If the music didn't come to him, alive inside his head, he would jar his head in between his knees and crouch within a corner on the back porch. He could then hear the distant melody of his vinyls. They'd taunt him as he edged closer to them, before the music disappeared altogether- drowned out by his mother and Lloyd's latest shouting match.

Then one day, the music moved from within his head and grew louder, on the other side of the house. He sprung up from his headlock, as the sharp call of the trumpet straightened his spine and knocked on his heart. He shook his head, to make sure the tune was not emanating from the chambers within his mind. It wasn't. It was real. It was here. He padded towards the uneven wooden fence, at the end of the yard, each step slower than the one before. There was a milli-second of silence in between the song which greeted him as an imposter of joy. He feared at any moment it may cut off. But as he tip-toed nearer, the momentary silences continued to be filled up with boisterous charges of the saxophone, double bass and drums. The piano tingled along in the background. But it was the trumpet that hypnotised him closer and closer towards the fence.

He dared to peek through the mini-holeon one of the planks. There it was. A vinyl player. No bigger, no smaller than the one he'd had to leave behind. It was yellow, unlike his beige one. The sight of that glorious vinyl of the Miles Davis Quintet and 'Round Midnight swivelling around, was soon blocked out by a pinkish, thinly veiled nightdress. The hole was fully blocked as an old lady leaned over the fence. Marvin barely caught a glimpse of her face as he swung around and cantered back towards the porch. There were not meant to be any humans in this vision. Even when he pictured the instruments in his mind, they were not being held by Miles Davis or any of the other geniuses who brought the song to life. It was just the melody and the melody alone. That was his background music.

He hurtled towards his room, forcing his mind to banish the idea of another person and her wrinkled hands resting on the fence and spoiling the music behind her. He crouched once more, this time in a corner in his room, willing the music to come back to him. He closed his eyes and swayed his head in between his knees. Slowly her face disappeared, even though he had barely looked the old lady in the eye. Soon, the floral patterns on her nightdress withered away before her whole body was gone. Finally, those hands unclawed themselves from the fence and his mind. And then there was only the music. 'Round Midnight. In all its unbound glory. His heart became steady once more; his orchestra of tranquillity playing out to his pace.

That evening, Lloyd strolled in, as he always did- on his own terms and unpredictable in his thought. Yet for a man who vibrated menacingly he was also a man that never drank. His sobriety did not fit the bill. He was abusive and unreliable- but not a drunk. A tea-totaller 'til the end. Marvin's mother,on the other hand, enjoyed her sherry. She drank to forget. She drank so that she could love. She drank without a glass- placing her lips directly on the bottle to ensure nothing went to waste. Even when Lloyd's palm struck her cheekbone, it did not matter. Sherry would bring her back to where she needed to go.

One day, Marvin stole a sip from the bottle. Never take from an alcoholic. They cannot remember anything, except where their next drink is coming from. And if they are robbed of that sip, there shall be no grace. Marvin's mother ought to have known how to master the slap by now. It was the only consistent action in her companionship with Lloyd. Yet when she hit her son, she could only graze his face with her hand knocking over the bottle. As it crashed onto the tiled kitchen floor, Marvin knew better than to stick around. His mother had become demonic having lost her real child that was now shards on the ground. She blocked the pathway to his room. The only other exit meant darting outside. As she edged towards him, he was off like jet-ski. He flung the outside door open and timing was kind to him. It sprung back just in time and smashed into his oncoming mother. She plummeted to the ground and stayed there. Not unconscious but rather distraught from spending a day without anymore sherry.
She howled for her son but Marvin moved further away. He panted and rested his palms on his thighs. It wasn't until he straightened back up that he realised where he was. He hesitated before taking a peek. This time, there was no vinyl player through the hole. The crisp air and moderate sun made for a perfect day, but without music none of it made sense. He turned back to the porch. Mother could no longer be heard. He wondered whether she still lay there or if she had indeed found another cold floor to shrivel on. He moved to head back to the house but felt a shadow over him.
  "What do you hear?"
  He did not answer her.
  "What do you hear, when there is no music to hear?"
  Marvin Baxter heard her words, then he heard the music in his head. He smiled at her and the old lady smiled back.
  "Come inside."
  She gracefully lifted him over the fence and then held his hand as she guided him into her house.

"I'm sorry. I don't have any soda. And I don't suppose you drink coffee or tea? Hmmm, maybe some water?"
Marvin was too busy gazing at the vinyl player, perched proudly on the mantle above the fireplace. What did drinks matter? What did anything else matter?

It was a big house for an old lady- especially an old lady alone. She thrust upon Marvin new geniuses he had not heard before. Al Green. Grover Washington Jr. John Coltrane. And in between, he wanted more of his new favourite. He kept gazing at the 'Round Midnight record, as a track from another vinyl was coming to an end. The old lady smiled and held up Miles Davis famous piece of work.

"Do you have a player at home?"

The boy shook his head, almost shamefully.

"No matter. Here. Take it. Listen, like you do. You don't need a player."

The boy grinned and gladly accepted the gift.

He rushed back that evening, with the record closely guarded to his chest. He laid it down gently, like a new-born, on his wooden room floor. He marvelled at the masterpiece for a while. Then he became bolder and removed it from its cover. He lightly traced his finger over the track rings on the vinyl, without touching them. And then it came to him again. The music in his head. Miles' saxophone beguiling him to leave reality once more. After that, he did not hear the crashing of a bottle onto the skull of a human head, downstairs. He continued to close his eyes and take in the bass, which made him oblivious to the sirens charging towards his house. As the piano gently caressed his brain waves and willed him to let go of any wariness, the noise from below his room did not reach him. He heard nothing but the background music.

Marvin fell asleep, vinyl by his side. In the morning, his stomach rumbled, having not had a single cracker the night before. He sluggishly made his way downstairs into an empty kitchen. His mother was not broodily sitting at the table. This morning, nothing but the growing sunlight, hit the sink. He wandered through the other rooms- all equally as lonely as the kitchen. Only one door was shut closed. His mother and Lloyd's room. He moved eerily closer, creaking on the floorboards as he neared the door. He looked up at the handle and reached for it. Before he could touch the brass lever, the door clicked open from the other side and slowly opened. There he stood, blankly looking at Marvin.

The policeman was a tall, thin man whose deadbeat face rendered him lifeless.

"Your mum is at the station."

Marvin looked at him and returned the blank gaze.

"She used a bottle of empty sherry to gash open her partner's head. He bled to death last night. It happened on the porch. I wouldn't advise going out there. We'll have someone around later to clean it up. Until then, we're trying to figure out whether it was self-defense from your mum. If it wasn't...well...you know..."

He stepped closer towards Marvin and hunched down before leaning in.

"Do you have anywhere to stay?"

Marvin's stomach rumbled. Did mother at least leave some marmalade in the fridge?

"Do you understand what I'm telling you?"

Marvin no longer cared for this man and casually turned his back on him to make his way toward the porch.

"My boy. Get back here!"

Marvin was able to drown out the background noise once more, as the music filled his head. The porch began to reek but had not yet reached its peak of decay. Fresh with murder it would not yet fully rot if the dull man inside kept his promise to Marvin. The music continued to play inside him and illuminated his path, through the semi-dry blood, to one place and one place only. Inside her house, the old lady made Marvin a peanut butter and jelly sandwich. And then another one, after he wolfed down the first. For dessert she knew what his little heart desired. She did not ask about his parents. Or whether they cared for his whereabouts. She merely got right down to it. Opening with Duke Ellington's majestic piano before moving onto Billie Holiday's hauntingly beautiful voice. Breakfast tuned into noon andthe music filled the house and weaved its way into the capsules that were their open souls. After she sliced up some fresh watermelon for him, the night was soon upon them.

Marvin's mother sat in the interrogation room, her left foot tapping impatiently against the table leg. Outside the room, two policemen discussed the mess that was Eliza Louise Baxter.

"I think she's delusional."

"What's this one's story?"

Claims she didn't do it. And has that crazy look in her eye. Where she actually believes it."

"Oh. And who does she think did it?"

"She's hysterically on about some old lady that came into her house late last night. Says she's never seen her before. Just started throttling her. The husband did nothing. He started laughing even. She broke free, grabbed the husband's truck keys and then ran for the porch. That kicked the man into action, who cannoned after her. Not before he grabbed the biggest knife in the kitchen. The old lady saw this and ran as well. This man had wretched luck, apparently. As his wife slammed the swinging door shut, it hit him hard. As he wobbled around, he sluggishly opened the door and made it to the porch. That's the furthest he got. The old lady promptly cracked the poor bastard on the head with a bottle of sherry. Wasn't the hit that killed him, his missus claims. But rather the way he cracked his head on the edge of the porch stairs."

"Really? She a doctor now?"

"Well our coronary just confirmed what she said. His neck cracked from steep downward movement. A fall rather than a blow."

The man shrugged his shoulders.

"I don't know. You believe any of this?"

"Would have liked to have asked the husband about her."

They both paused, then laughed heartily.

"Crazy damn neighbourhood. By the way, how was this called in?"

"Dave said some lady phoned the station. Mrs Baxter claims she called it in. But the lady didn't sound hysterical. So, you see. She's full of it."

"And what time did this happen."

"Hmmm let's see here. Aaaah yes. 'Round midnight or so."

Javi Reddy has spent most of his career within the business communications realm, as a Communications Manager. He has written on various platforms within a corporate environment. His career has seen him work at companies such as IBM; the Shoprite Group and Telesure Investment Holdings, whilst also freelancing for a few sporting and entertainment publications. Aside, from being the Grand Prize Winner in the Eyelands Magazine short story contest, his story 'Sit Down; You're Brown' was awarded runner-up in the 'The SA Writers College 2019 Annual Short Story Competition'. His debut novel, 12 Yards Out, will soon be released after being handled by a UK publishing house. Javi lives in Johannesburg, South Africa.

PRIZES
(by submission order)
Midnight shadows
David McVey

Everybody hates me, thought Kyle, just because my hair sticks up in that funny way and I'm shy of girls and I haven't had a job since I left college.

Kyle had snaffled a good handful of his mum's stash of sleeping pills; enough to do the job, anyway. But what about the mess, the scene? He'd probably puke before dying and if it got on the carpet or bedclothes mum would be raging. And she'd hate all the hassle - police, ambulance, undertakers. How much did a funeral cost nowadays? Even if nobody came?

And then Kyle thought about Derryburn Wood. Nobody went there except dog-walkers and daft wee boys who wanted to get drunk and there would be nobody there at night. He could slip out, find a hidden spot, pop the pills and die quietly. No one would be inconvenienced, no one would mind the mess.

It was nearly twelve and there was a bright moon. Kyle pulled on a capacious hoodie, transferred the sleeping pills to a pocket and took a bottle of spring water to wash them down. He was about to leave the bedroom for the last time when he noticed that the duvet, which he'd been lying on, was crinkled and untidy. Mum would go mental. He shook it smooth before creeping quietly downstairs in case he woke her, and then disappeared into the cooling night to die in Derryburn Wood.

A ship of light swept over the horizon of the dark, trailing a wake of silence. Jane had missed the last bus.

It had already been a hard evening, involving what Sally from work had called a 'break-up date'. She had arranged to meet Scott in a charmless chain pub called the Goblet and Wishbone on an edge-of-town trading estate. While Scott fetched the drinks, Jane had reflected on the meanness of her reason for ending things: Scott was just too nice.

He held doors open for her. He bought her flowers (too many - some bunches went straight into the green bin). He was open about his feelings and considerate about hers. He loved children; before long there'd be a marriage proposal with a view to starting a family. He was generous, sharing, thoughtful, someone who wanted to share his life - fruitfully - with someone else.

Jane didn't. Not yet, anyway. Scott was 30, which explained a lot. She was still only 24 and wanted the free, fun-loving life a bit longer. And yet, even when she told Scott the cold truth, he had managed to be gracious.

'I didn't see this coming,' he had said, with the puzzled facial expression of a gentle forest creature that had misplaced some nuts, 'but I appreciate your honesty and courage in telling me.'

Get angry, Jane had thought. Why do you never get angry?

Scott left soon afterwards but Jane had remained behind, drinking. Only when the last bus was due to abandon this desolate urban periphery did she emerge, only to see it disappearing down the ring-road. Bus drivers just want to get home too, she thought. She'd drunk a lot and it moved her to be reasonable. Like Scott.

She considered phoning for a taxi, but it was a dry, breezy night in May - the sun had barely gone down - and while it was a long way by road to her home on the Glenturlie Estate it was just a mile or so through countryside. A footpath ran from the ring-road between fields to Derryburn Wood; soon after the path re-emerged from the wood, you saw the first houses of the estate. There was a moon riding high in the sky and surely on a Tuesday night there would be no feral fourteen-year-olds giggling round a bottle of tonic wine in some dark corner? She clicked across the ring-road in her heels and crunched onto the gravel farm track that marked the beginning of the path.

Revd Rab Soutar needed to pray. He needed God to hear him, and to know that he had been heard. There was always something unsatisfying about praying in the manse; nothing to do with Carol or the children, just the sense of being enclosed. A ceiling wouldn't prevent words reaching an omnipotent God but it could inhibit the person doing the praying.

Glenturlie Parish Church was a pleasing modern building of plain harling with some pinewood panels; large windows in the ceiling brought the sun into the morning service. The estate it served was large, sprawling and rich. The church was rich, too; Rab ministered to lawyers and GPs and lecturers and high-powered IT execs, their wives, husbands and children. There were always funds for repairs to the church building or crèche equipment. But Rab tried to open the congregation's hearts and minds to mission, to bringing Christ to the lost, to serving the poor and despairing and hungry. There were many needy folk, locally, albeit on the other side of town. His sermons were met with nods and smiles but little else. The church was determined to keep its hands clean.

Rab craved prayer. He would go to a quiet spot in Derryburn Wood and pour out his soul to the Lord, seeking His will for Revd Rab Soutar and for Glenturlie Parish Church. He would pray also that God would lead him, personally, to troubled souls that he could help.

The moon blinked between trees as Rab entered the wood. Away from the sodium-bathed streets, darkness embraced him and stars upon stars gleamed from the velvety sky, an infinity of tiny lights that spoke to him of the limitless,

12

unimaginable reach of God. He decided to pray where a small patch of grass bounded the path. He took off his Craghopper cagoule, laid it on the ground, and knelt on it.

'This is SHITE!' yelled Jason, hurling a newly-emptied lager can into the unseen undergrowth. 'It's dark. We cannae see anything. What are we doing here, man?'

'Chill, man, I just thought it would be cool,' said Connor, 'all spooky and that. I didnae think it would be so cold and dark.'

Jason softened when Connor admitted his error. 'It'll be a magic place to come when we plunk off school, though. Naebody from the council will find us here.'

Connor detached the plastic carrier bag of drink from the branch on which he'd hung it and they began to pick their way along the path using the faint light from their mobiles. Then Jason stopped. 'That's weird, man. Do you hear that?'

'What?'

'Somebody. Talking.'

'Naw. No at this time of night, surely...'

The path led past some pine trees to an open glade wanly lit by the moon. Just off the path they sensed a dark, stooping figure - no, a kneeling figure - muttering away to himself. 'Show me your will... lead me in your ways... soften our hearts towards the weak...'

'He's mental,' whispered Connor.

'It's pure scary, man, let's go.'

They ignored the path and clattered off through the trees. Dimly, they saw the lights of the Glenturlie Estate and ran towards them, the branches clawing as they went. They only stopped running when they reached a scruffy field bordering the estate.

'I left the bag,' said Connor.

'What?'

'The bag with the drink. I dropped it when we saw the mad guy.'

'This was a great idea.' Jason trudged away towards the lights of town.

This is life, Jane thought as she entered the wood. She was warm from the gentle climb through the fields but it felt good. Pity about her shoes; they were ruined. She switched on her mobile to light the path a little.

Kyle inhaled the mouldy breath of the wood. There was peace, here, quietness. And then, just ahead of him, he heard a muffled tattoo of running feet on the soft woodland floor. Two shadows fled past through sparely-filtered moonlight.

Not far along, on the same path, he saw something bright that shifted and crinkled gently in the breeze; a plastic bag. He picked it up and peered inside; a half-full bottle of Buckfast and a few cans of multipack lager. Well, they'll help, Kyle thought, they'll deaden the pain.

More footsteps, behind him this time. They stopped.

He turned to see a young woman, wearing a light raincoat over a short dress, and smart, high-heeled shoes. He edged closer to get a clearer view.

'Don't hurt me,' said Jane.

'It's all right,' said Kyle, 'I won't.' He nodded at the plastic bag. 'This isn't mine. I found it.'

He sounded nice, thought Jane, well-spoken. What a shame he was out on his own, drinking. 'I'd better be getting along,' she said.

'Yes. Midnight walk?'

'Yes. Just going home.'

He watched as she disappeared into the gloom. Even struggling with those heels, there was a grace about her. If she was to be the last person he'd ever see, he hadn't chosen badly.

He crawled into the midst of a cluster of rhododendrons and felt in his pockets for the tablets. He sat on a dry stump of wood, remembering that mum always said you could catch something from sitting on something damp. He reached into the carrier bag for a can and wished he hadn't brought the water. It seemed a waste, now.

Rab stood up and retrieved his cagoule. A night of victorious prayer. Now and then he had heard voices, whisperings, the sound of passing feet. Distractions sent by the Enemy? If so, they had failed. Rab glanced at his watch; quarter to one. The night would soon be compromised by the first dirty grey light. He set off for the manse.

Connor followed Jason into the Glenturlie estate, where all the poshies lived, but then turned towards the path that led back into Derryburn Wood. He couldn't leave that drink behind.

Just as he entered the wood he met an attractive young woman who was coming the other way. Ignoring his 'Hi, doll!' she continued speaking into her mobile; 'I'm sorry to phone so late, Scott, and I'm sorry about tonight. Can I see you tomorrow?' Lucky Scott, whoever he was; she had nice legs and that, though she shouldn't have walked through the wood in those heels.

He hadn't gone much further when he met a middle-aged man wearing a cagoule and a tweed bunnet. They both stopped.

'Can I help you, young man? I'm Revd Soutar of Glenturlie Parish Church.'

'Aye. Have ye seen a plastic bag somebody might have dropped?'

Kyle lay down; the damp didn't worry him, now. He just felt warmth and peace and silence as the faint smell of rhododendron blossom fought with the mouldiness. He was hidden from sight in this lonely woodland place. Would anyone ever find him?

The minister guy had tried to convert Connor so he had pulled away and scampered into the wood. When he got back to the place there was no sign of the carry-out but at least the mad guy had gone. A strong gust of wind blew in from somewhere, penetrating even the sheltered places, the kind of wind you got at scary bits in horror films. Behind those big bushes, something rustled. A plastic bag?

There were steely bars of light in the sky now but it was still deep-dark among the bushes. There was his carry-out, though. Someone had definitely been at it, just two cans left and no sign of the Buckie.

Connor turned and saw something dark and still on the ground. He looked at the silent shape for a long time and wondered what it was. The light seemed a long way away.

David McVey *lectures in Communication at New College Lanarkshire. He has published over 120 short stories and a great deal of non-fiction that focuses on history and the outdoors. He enjoys hillwalking, visiting historic sites, reading, watching telly, and supporting his home-town football team, Kirkintilloch Rob Roy FC.*

PRIZE
At Last, Goodbye
Wendy Craig

Dear Yianni

I am writing this at Eleftherios Venizelos airport. My flight leaves Athens in an hour; I'll be landing in England late tonight. The lounge at the boarding gate is full. Some people look nervous, some bored. Some are alight with excitement, perhaps delighted to be going on holiday or anticipating a reunion with a loved one. Me, I feel numb.

It's four months now since your Uncle Theo came to see me one night. It was late, around midnight. I had just got into bed. I wasn't expecting a knock on the door at that time. Then to see him standing there, his face so grave, I knew it must be bad news. About you.

'Agapeti mou, my dear,' he said, his voice breaking.

'Come in, come in,' I said, my eyes searching his face, noting his grief. 'Is it Yiannis?'

Uncle Theo didn't reply. He walked straight through my apartment and out onto the balcony.

It was a fine night, still warm, and there was a full moon. Yianni, remember how we used to stand, arms round each other, and watch the full moon rise on those nights we were together. For me it was always a special time. You told me once the legend of the moon goddess, Selene; how she drove her chariot across the sky each night, on her way to visit her lover, the shepherd Endymion. I always liked listening to you when you talked of the gods and goddesses, the heroes and oracles. You knew so much. You could quote Herodotus and Homer as well as your favourite writer Hemingway, Aristotle and Aeschylus as well as my favourite Apollinaire. That is what I was thinking when I went to sit beside Uncle Theo in the moonlight over the harbour.

I waited for him to speak. He was gazing out at the Chania lighthouse, watching its white light flick around, illuminating the sea wall and the old buildings edging that little semi-circle of the Venetian Harbour

'I have brought pomegranates, your favourite,' he said.

And of course that made me think of you too, Yianni. I remember the first time you gave me one, that beautiful pink and crimson streaked ball. I wanted to stroke its smooth skin, to gaze at every detail of its subtle, rich colour. It was then you told me the legend of Persephone.

Out gathering poppies one day she was abducted by Hades and taken to the Underworld. Demeter, the Corn Goddess, wandered the earth searching for her daughter, plunging the land into winter. She, in her despair, forbad the crops to bear fruit. Finally Zeus stepped in and proclaimed that Persephone would, if she had not eaten anything while in the Underworld, be allowed to return to her distraught mother. But crafty Hades did not give up his bride so easily. He handed her a pomegranate. She must have held it as I did then, caressed it, smelt it, and been overcome by temptation. Her fate was sealed. It was only after the intercession of the goddess Hecate that Persephone was permitted to go back to the world, but not for the whole year. When it is winter, she is back with Hades.

I broke open the glowing ball with my thumbs, as Uncle Theo had his. Inside, sheathed in a fine creamy casing, lay rows of sweet pink pearls like jewels in a velvet-lined casket. I picked one out and felt it explode in a burst of cold sweetness as I bit it. Then another and another till I was eating them quickly and their juice was running pink down my arm. But this time I took no pleasure from eating the pomegranate. I don't think Uncle Theo did either. And I was stricken by a sudden, horrifying thought. Had he brought me this particular fruit as a sign that Yiannis was dead?

At last Uncle Theo began. 'Claudette ...' and he wept.

'Is he dead?' I asked

Your uncle, my guardian angel raised his eyebrows and tipped his head back in that Greek way of saying «ochi», no.

I realised I was holding my breath. My hands were clenched so tightly my fingernails cut into my palms. 'Then what? What can be so bad?'

'He was struck by a car yesterday as he was crossing the street, outside the university's Faculty of Medicine. He had been lecturing there, about the research he was doing into brain function. According to witnesses, he was flung into the air and came down heavily, striking his head on the edge of the kerb. An ambulance came within minutes and he was taken straight to hospital. His mother phoned me an hour ago. Yiannis has broken bones – they will heal. But he has brain damage and is in an induced coma. The doctors are not certain of the outcome but suspect, because of the area of the brain that was impacted, that he may suffer catastrophic memory loss.'

I couldn't take it all in. I didn't understand. 'What does that mean?' I asked.

'That he won't remember anything, long or short term. He won't remember who I am, who you are, what you've done, where you've been. He won't remember that you were once lovers, that you love him. Nothing, Claudette. Nothing.'

I cried then. Uncle Theo stood and bent to hold me while I sobbed. After a little while he patted me on the shoulder and left. I sat out there on the balcony as the moon moved across the sky. As the lighthouse flicked, flicked, flicked its beam. As the sky turned from midnight dark to dawn light, from black to gold, as the sun rose in a glow of fire.

A quotation by Aeschylus slipped into my mind.

'There is no pain as great as the memory of joy in present grief.'

17

I wept again. I thought of us. I thought of all our shared memories of joy which would now be mine alone. I was grieving, Yianni. I had lost you once when you married. Now I had lost you again.

I phoned Uncle Theo two days later, asking him to meet me at our favourite restaurant beside the harbour.

'There's no more news of Yiannis,' he said, anticipating my first question. 'His condition is no different. It's very serious. If he does survive he will not be the same man we have known. He will be changed.' The tears in his eyes mirrored my own. 'Go back to England, Claudette. Go back to your own country. Without Yiannis, Greece cannot hold you any longer.'

'I have been without Yiannis for six years,' I replied. 'Since he married Renia.'

'But you still love him. You still hope.'

I looked into the concerned, caring face of that dear man who had become my friend and guardian angel and all I could say was, 'Yes.'

So, Yianni, over the course of the last three months I have dismantled my life in Chania. I gave up my apartment in the Old Town with its view of the lighthouse. I resigned from my job. The tenants who had been renting my mother's house in London since she died left last week. I will be reclaiming it as my home. My Greek friends gave me a raucous going away party. When anyone asked why I was returning to England, I would just say, 'It's time.'

I know you won't remember this, Yianni. I came to your apartment to see you before I left for the airport this afternoon. It was six years since I'd been in that building but I found my way as if I were a homing pigeon. Nothing in the area had changed.

But I was shocked by the changes in you and your apartment. Your hair was cut very short. That lock that used to flop over your forehead, the one I liked to smooth to one side, had been trimmed right away. You looked like an older and thinner version of Yiannis, you sounded like Yiannis but it was as if the essence of you had disappeared. Your eyes were dull.

'Who is it?' you asked.

'It's Claudette.'

'How do I know you?'

'We're old friends,' I said. 'I lived in Chania.'

'Come in then. Sit down. Renia's out.'

Your apartment used to be sparsely furnished with high quality pieces. I'd always found it restful. Now Renia's influence was everywhere. Your masculine black leather couches had been replaced by chintzy armchairs and a clashing floral sofa. Strips of white crocheted triangles edged the open shelves. An embroidered tablecloth covered the small dining table. I imagined her mother and aunties had prepared traditional items like these for her dowry. There were photos of you

18

and Renia, of Renia and her parents, of your marriage ceremony on every available surface. I wondered how you, with your almost monk-like asceticism, felt about the clutter.

So we chatted, Yianni, about the weather, the holidays, my job, but it was as strangers. 'Renia's out,' you said again. You told me you were having treatment for your back injuries. How you hoped to be able to walk without crutches in another couple of months.

'Are you in any pain?" I asked.

'Yes,' you said, and then lapsed into silence. Our conversation died. It was as if I wasn't there.

'Renia's out,' you repeated.

'I'll go now,' I said. 'I just wanted to see you before I flew to Britain.'

Your reply was formal. 'Thank you for coming. Kalo taxidhi, have a good trip.'

When I stood up to leave we didn't hug or kiss. You held out your hand. I shook it.

'I'll let myself out,' I said. 'Go well, Yianni. Goodbye.'

The door banged open and Renia burst in. She looked as surprised to see me as I was to see her appear so suddenly.

'Ti kanei edo, (what's she doing here?)' she demanded of you, her mouth twisting sideways in an ugly expression of contempt, her words scattering like machine gun fire. I answered in Greek which surprised her. How often had that happened with your countrymen, Yianni? We used to joke about it, how my blonde hair made them think the only Greek I'd know would be the few phrases tourists use – hello, goodbye, please, thank you, yia sou, adio, parakalo, efcharisto. Very few expected me to speak fluently. 'I'm going back to England,' I said. 'I came to say goodbye.'

She put her arm round your shoulder in a possessive gesture, laid her other hand, fingers splayed, on your chest. 'Don't let us keep you,' she said. I said goodbye then to you both and walked away, down that long corridor to the elevator. Goodbye for the last time.

Before I left for the airport I did three things, Yianni. I went to one of the shops in Apollonos Street, near the cathedral. The shop had a claustrophobic feel, crammed as it was with shelves and shelves of religious Orthodox icons, trays of blue glass beads in many sizes to ward off the Evil Eye, embossed silver frames, hanging brass lamps and chandeliers. There were boards pinned with dozens of those little, rectangular votive offerings made of tin. Amongst all the tamata (offerings) with their images of body parts, babies, men, women, children, houses, even cars and cows, I found one of a head and one that simply said efcharisto, thank you.

From there I made my way to the street where the stores, lined cheek by jowl, sell sewing requirements. I used to love going there when I had spare time in

Athens. Sorting through the racks of ribbons, all displayed by colour, to find just the right shade; choosing unusual buttons for a sewing project. I bought a metre of navy blue, thin ribbon and asked the saleslady to cut it in half. She watched as I threaded a length through the hole in each tama and nodded her approval. The third task was to go to the chapel behind the university. Students were popping in and out of the small, simple building, on their way to lectures to kiss an icon, to light a candle. The cleaning lady was taking spent candles from the bins and replacing them with new beeswax tapers. She didn't seem to worry about all the noise she made, the clattering and clanging as she rattled round.

Yianni, I strung up the tamata by their ribbons underneath a silver framed icon. The one with the head was for you, to invoke a miracle for the healing of your brain injury and restoration of your memory. The one of thanks was for you too, and for Uncle Theo, and Chania and Greece. Thanks for the last ten years of my life. Then I lit a candle and hailed a cab to take me to the airport.

Of all our goodbyes over the four years of our love affair, of all our comings and goings between my home in Chania and yours in Athens, this farewell was the easiest for me. Because, Yianni, this time I had given up hope. This time really is goodbye.

The last call for boarding has been announced. I must go. I should be back home in England around midnight.

Claudette

Wendy Craig first visited Greece in 1974 and has returned many times. From 1990 to 2014 Wendy combined her love of travel, history and making miniature models to contribute articles to newspapers, magazines and an internet-based magazine. She was a newspaper columnist with a fortnightly column 'Back in Time' on Auckland history. She wrote a humorous monthly column called 'Wendy's World' in the British The Dolls' House Magazine. Her work has appeared in the New Zealand Herald, Christchurch Press, Otago Daily Times, Suburban Newspapers, Australian Women's Weekly, Holiday, More Magazine, Hostelling Horizon, Travel Trade and The Dolls House Magazine among others.

PRIZE
The Banshee's Sister
E. F. S. Byrne

Familiar cries wailed out as I tossed the salads and checked the oven. Whose turn was it now was all I could wonder, shivering in the hail. A car crunched on the drive. They were beginning to arrive. I sighed.

She never stopped screeching, my sister, my twin sister. She punched, kicked and bit, claiming it was me making all the noise.

Even as a baby, I could sense our parents going crazy. They had five other children. We were the final couple, little girls, long red hair screaming and blaring, clambering for attention. The others crumbled over our cot, vultures, little dragons breathing fire, tickling us with their fingers, their jealous needs.

It is no fun being the baby, babies in a family. Brothers and sisters crowd you out. No matter how pretty and confident they tell you to be, you flare up and blow away into the corner, cobwebs gluing your eyelids together as people chatter, trundle around, ignoring your presence, absence, lack of ambition. It's worse when you live in a castle: plenty of room to be lost in, ignored, put into cold storage while elder siblings rule the roost, hold fort, keep the rabble at bay.

I was first born, first out of the womb. That's what I always told my little sister. She would look at me with those big brown eyes, stare into mine, mirrors bubbling with affection and revenge. I tell her. She nods. Smiles. Runs off playfully. I follow. Because, really, no matter how much I hate her, we can't be apart. And she knows that, which is why she won't let me go.

My brothers manage hedge funds, my sister the Supreme Court. Us baby twins were left with the house, the grounds, and the responsibility of keeping our heritage from falling in around us.

The stonewall, the turret, the hills have begun to groan under the weight of rocks, the river under the stench of silage and poorly irrigated milking parlours. I remember a sturdy mound jutting out into time but now it's our inheritance, crumbling with age, struggling to breathe under the weight of dark, damp stones fitted unevenly together.

It remains a symbol of what our family name stood for. We still meet here, at least once a year. Perched on the hill, overlooking our personal mound of rocky crevices, those roughly hewn feelings that were strung together to create a castle, the family abode, continue to reign. No one ever checked the foundations, the boggy soil before they started building. Every year it sinks a little more, the Keep less imposing, slouching, sulking ominously in the winterly winds, the beat of time in search of a destiny.

After my parents died we began to return to the howling walls, pretending we loved the place, ourselves. We extended our families in search of succour and drew new members into the poisoned ivy that was our upbringing, my mother screaming, my father drinking and then the opposite as they got older. When they hit out at us we ran for cover. Sitting at the battered, oak table, slurping bitter wine, sometimes I close my eyes and remember all the hiding places, damp, slippery steps behind the fireplace, the spooky trapdoor that led to the hays heds, the twisting stairwell that ran up to the tower which was always locked with a chain.

For good reason. Only my mother had the key, which is why she was the first to throw herself from the thin parapet and break her neck in the dried out moat. My sister wailed for days, her voice capturing centuries of weeping, family lore, the remorse bad luck strokes into an eternal flame. People said we were cruel landlords; we deserved every blow the surname received. We didn't agree. We mourned each loss. My sister couldn't stop crying. When Dad missed his footing on the twisted stairwell step up the tower we did wonder, if the castle itself had feeling, was vengeful.

I can hear my sister sobbing, screaming, screeching into the tangled night sky, through the empty wind that folds her cries and bundles them along, over the mountain ranges, under my pillow, through my brain.

My little twin sister. I can see her face before me along the crumbling battlements. I hate the way she loves us, keeps telling us we are doing it all wrong and then bleating through the night when we prove her right.

Wild red salmon and pale, pink turkey should be enough to keep us going, no matter who turns up at the table. Another family meal. I don't know how many places to set. I don't know if she is dead or alive. My ears ring, burn with the heat of the fireplace. I can still taste her tears on my cheeks, her fingers tracing the outline of my nose, every day, just after midnight, when the crying starts.

Enda Scott (E. F. S. Byrne): *Dedicated to education and being a father, E. F. S. Byrne has finally found more time to devote to his writing and is currently working on everything from very short flash stories to full-length novels. Samples and links to over thirty published stories can be read at efsbyrne.wordpress.com or follow him on Twitter @efsbyrne*

PRIZE
Crying all the way to the bank
Karen Keeley

She was crying all the way to the bank, telling me we didn't have any money, it was all gone. She kept yanking on my arm, trying to get me to let go—but I had a firm grip. I smiled, told her banks had oodles of money, why shouldn't we get a slice of the pie?

"You're insane, Rocko!" she kept hollering. "I'm telling you, the money is all gone!"

"That's okay," I told her. "There's always plenty more. Ask and you shall receive."

"But there's nothing to receive!"

"Watch and learn, Marta—watch and learn." By then we'd reached the bank. I'd finished my smoke, flicked the butt to the curb and shoved Marta in through the front entrance, double glazed doors, left side locked, right side open, "push here," and there we were, standing inside the bank.

I let loose with the AK-47, shot the ceiling full of holes, an art deco design with swirls and geometric shapes, plaster and glass raining down. The bank was on Columbia Street in New Westminster right by the river. I figured the art deco ceiling was a given, the bank built back in the twenties, the time of F. Scott Fitzgerald and Charles Lindberg flying the Atlantic. Now there was a guy with class and guts. Too bad what happened to his kid.

What with the noise and the volley of bullets, I got everyone's attention—customers and customer service reps, bank manager, too. He came running, an intellectual geek in his thirties, probably a numbers guy, eyes wide, mop of dark hair dishevelled, who in the name of Christ was setting off firecrackers in his bank? Only it wasn't Halloween, no firecrackers. Just me with the AK-47, hell of a firearm, shoots thirty rounds per minute.

I shoved Marta toward the counter. "You know what to do."

She was crying as she handed the duffle bag to the first of the customer service reps, her too, crying. You'd think the two of them were at a goddamn wake what with all the fussing and blubbering and hand wringing.

I hollered, "Everyone on the floor!" and bodies dropped like bowling pins knocked down in a weekend tournament. People lay there weeping and wailing—they had families, little kids, wives and husbands at home or at work. Me too, I was thinking. I had a family too, and I meant to take care of them.

Why couldn't Marta see that? I was doing this for her and the kids. We needed money, Christ—the whole world needed money and most of it squirrelled away in the goddamn banks, as if those mega-financial institutions didn't already make enough dough, what with their customer service fees, returns on investments, sky high mortgage interest rates.

I should know, I worked at a bank once upon a time, a loan's officer until the recession hit and I was given my pink slip. "Sorry, Rocko—times are tough, we gotta cut back."

Cut back! Jesus—they'd slit my wrists expecting Marta and me to make a go of it on lousy EI benefits which ran out in less than a year and no other jobs to be had.

Well, I'd show 'em. We'd take the money and run, just like I'd been telling Marta, we were starting over, a clean slate, a new town, a new province—we could choose the Maritimes or one of the three territories in Canada's north, land of the midnight sun. If it could happen for those in witness protection, why not us? We needed protection, too. It couldn't be that hard to get a new identity. Identity theft—it happened all the time. Just read the papers, listen to the news or go online to all those social media sites, always someone bitchin' about identity theft. How hard could it be?

She was crying all the way to the precinct, the two of us handcuffed and locked in the back of the police cruiser. She kept trying to tell the cop who was driving she was an unwitting accomplice. More like dimwitted, I was thinking—her too slow with the money bag. She'd taken too long to get the damn thing filled and someone in the bank set off the silent alarm.

Maybe if Marta hadn't fainted we'd have gotten out of there sooner. Low blood sugar, she said. Dehydrated, she said. Earlier I'd given her our last twenty bucks, sent her to the store for some food but she came back with a bottle of Jack Daniel's and a pack of cigarettes, a little pick-me-up, she'd said, something to take the sting out of our meager existence. The Police cars too, arrived without the use of sirens so when we eventually ran from the bank, there they were, a dozen cop cars circling the bank like a covered wagon surrounded by an Apache war party, back in the days of Jesse James. Now there too, was a guy with class and guts, robbing banks, robbing trains, what was called guerrilla warfare tactics in those days. I still held the AK-47 and thought about good old Jesse, ripping a volley of bullets through the posse but I knew before I'd even pulled the trigger, they'd let fire with their own arsenal of weapons.

Marta and I didn't stand a chance.

Stupid, bitch—too goddamn slow what with all the crying and the fainting and now blubbering in the back seat of the cop car. "He made me do it!" gobs of snot running from her nose, her eyes all red and puffy. "He said he'd hurt me—me and the kids. I had to go along with his plan."

"Save it for your lawyer," snarled the cop driving.

I wanted to punch Marta in the face but I figured that would only hurt my defense, prove I was a menace, a threat to others. I asked if I could smoke, guy

24

driving said it was a no smoking vehicle. Hell—government didn't have a problem taking the taxes. So much for legitimate enterprises, us smokers treated like goddamn pariahs by the righteous non-smokers. I gazed out the window and watched the buildings fly by, caught a sliver of the Fraser River in the distance, another guy with class and guts, Simon Fraser, explorer and fur trader and the first white guy to follow the river from its source in the Rocky Mountains to the Pacific Ocean. Gotta admire a guy like that. Business folks too, strolling free as you please on the sidewalks, some meandering along and others pressed for time, another goddamn meeting. The dogs too, were sniffing the fire hydrants and then lifting a leg. I figured they were telling the world, piss on it. All I wanted was the money. Was that so hard to understand? Money made the world go round. Without it you're nothing, just another piece of dog shit on somebody's shoe. Dog shit scraped onto the sidewalk or the curb, stinkin' up the environment. It now appeared my environment was going to be the inside of a goddamn jail cell.

She was crying all the way to the courthouse, to the arraignment. We were represented by council, some geeky kid wearing thick tortoiseshell glasses, pimples on his forehead doing penance or some such thing—community service, he called it. The kid's suit looked like it came from goodwill, too large, too ill fitting. Maybe he was strapped for cash, bogged down with student loans, fresh out of law school. The kid said he could likely get Marta off but he wasn't so sure about me. I, after all, had the firearm, a goddamn AK-47 assault rifle. And Marta's story did sound plausible. I had forced her to go with me to the bank. I did admit that much. But hell, she was my wife, in it for better or worse, in sickness and in health. I admit, I had a sickness. Sick of running from one flop house to another, sick of skipping out on the rent, two kids in tow, little guys only three and four years old, what kind of a life was that for them? They should've been in pre-school or play-school or whatever it is little kids do, not pushing Dinky Toy cars around on a cold linoleum floor in the kitchen because there was no money for heat or play-time activities.

Marta said she could've gone back to trickin' but I wasn't having any of that. That's where I'd met her, on the street when I was the high and mighty loan's officer at the bank. Had lots of money in those days, enough to pay for a piece of tail once a week. Then something happened, I fell in love with the bitch. Or at least, I told myself it was love. Asked her to marry me, get her off the street, into a home, we'd start a family, be normal folk living in a three bedroom brick bungalow, double glazed windows, a swing set in the backyard. I wanted a working fire hydrant on the corner, a monkey tree in the front yard. We had all that for a while, first Luke, then Logan. Had a dog too, found her at the SPCA and then she got hit by a car. I thought Marta's crying would bring down the heavenly angels to resurrect the silly mutt but that didn't happen. Dog laid there deader than a doornail. Guy driving—him too, crying and sniveling. No class, no guts with that guy. What followed was the loss of my job. Jesus! Life on a downhill slide. But I wasn't having Marta selling her tail on the street. A man's got his dignity, his self-respect to consider. And the boys. No matter how little they were, they'd understand something was up if their Momma was gone all hours at night, me drinking Jack Daniels earlier in the day and then switching to cheap bourbon later on, always money for the booze and the cigarettes but no money for the food or the bills. Even so, I'd told Marta, forget the idea of selling her tail on the street, no sirree!

She was crying all the way to the bank except this time they were tears of happiness. She'd been bangin' the bank manager, the intellectual geek in his thirties. While she was robbing the tills, he was robbing the accounts. A cool million wired to an untraceable account on the Isle of Crete. It's always round midnight I find myself thinking—how did I miss the bank manager? I know I saw him at the start, right after I pulled the trigger and striated that art deco ceiling with a dozen rounds from the AK-47, plaster and glass raining down. I was sure he was on the floor whimpering and sniveling with the others.

Marta must have distracted me what with all that crying and then the customer service reps crying. Jesus! Women and their goddamn tears and the waterworks allowed the bank manager to slip away. The missing money was blamed on me—as though I'd pulled a Houdini and hidden it before I'd skedaddled out of the bank.

"Are you nuts?" I told my lawyer. "Do I look like Houdini?"

"You tell me," he said, shoving his glasses up the bridge of his nose. I wanted to punch him in the face. Would have too, if it hadn't have been for the guard. He had a nasty weapon strapped to his hip along with a Billy-club and a Taser. Those guards don't fool around.

The court was told I had the computer skills, what with the previous job as a loan's officer, the untraceable account set up in Marta's maiden name, Karavitas, if you can believe that, an alias for me. The Judge took a hissy fit, called it grand larceny and identity theft. He then went totally ballistic when Queen's council said I'd left the boys in the car, sleeping like babies, tanked up on Benadryl. My explanation, both boys sick with colds, tubes in their ears but the Judge wasn't buying any of it, called it reckless abandon of a minor. He sentenced me five to ten, without parole. He certainly was a hard ass that goddamn Judge.

I'm the one that should be crying. Can't smoke in jail either. Clean air act, I'm told. My boys are with social services and me facing jail time. The Judge didn't take kindly to my using the AK-47. He said I had it coming, scaring all those people, I was a goddamn menace. If justice was to be served, he certainly wasn't about to give a rat's ass that it was my first offence.

But Marta, she played it up good, the terrified victim, the wife of a crazy man. Judge felt sorry for her. Of course, she'd dolled herself up like a penitent nun, think Sophia Loren in that movie White Sister. That probably helped, too. When Marta played a role, she played it good. For me, it had been baby-doll—Christ, that got me everytime. She'd pout and then suck on a goddamn candy soother as big as a Popsicle. How could I not get aroused, a move like that. My pecker with a mind of its own.

The bank manager, I wonder what role she played for him. The gangster's moll? Wouldn't put it past her and now, the two of them are on Crete, drinking strawberry ouzitos sportin' those teeny tiny corrugated umbrellas. I figure she's enjoying dried figs as an appetizer, black olives, too. Marta always said black olives were rich with antioxidants. Gotta love those olives—and the money too, wired to some untraceable account—used the dark web, I'm sure. Marta got off Scott free, double jeopardy, I'm told, nothing they could do and besides, they're still certain it was me what did the dirty deed, an untraceable financial transaction. And why wouldn't they believe Marta? Her so convincing when she told her side of the story, a real class act, was Marta—me, disappearing for those five minutes, leaving her to watch the others."I had too, your honour. He threatened my boys! I was afraid for our lives!" followed by more tears. Didn't the bitch realize I was doing it for her?

I wasn't fiddling with any goddamn computer, I was clearing out the safe in the basement, no time code on that baby, a Leopold bank vault built in the twenties.

I hope Marta gets good and sunburned, her little tush blistered and peeling.

I hope her goddamn skin falls off.

That too, would get her crying if she lost her looks. Her identity is tied to her looks. If Marta ever had to rely on her brains, she'd be in major trouble—too thinned skinned, too emotional and dumber than a doorknob. Hell, thinking smart has never been Marta's forté.

Karen Keeley is a former Communications Analyst with the Yukon government, having lived in Whitehorse, Yukon for many years. Her short fiction has appeared in literary journals and two anthologies, Flying Colours and Gush, menstrual manifestos for our times. Darkhouse Books recently accepted a short story for a mystery anthology to be published in the fall 2019. She is now retired and makes her home in Calgary, Alberta, Canada.

SHORT LIST
(by submission order)
Belonging
Judith Diamond

March 3, 1892
My name is Ava Isabella Calhoun, and I now have attained my 25th year. Before time descends like a fog, blurring all memory, I wish to set forth the story of my aunt, Sylvie Calhoun. Our families' homes sit just back of the riverbank in Pine Ridge, Virginia. Sylvie's father, my grandfather, Hank Calhoun, was an industrious, red-bearded farmer who had migrated here from a hardscrabble, Allegheny mountain town.His wife, Annie Petrelis, followed her family from an island in Greece to Florida and then to Virginia, searching for land to farm. Hank and Anniemet, married and set down their rootsin Pine Ridge. First a boy, Peter, arrived; six years later, Sylvie. People around this place trust their relatives and those who have a history of generations in the town. Hank wasn't born here. Annie still had a trace of an accent. The children would have found acceptance difficult no matter how they were.

Peter was a quiet, studious child. Sylvie was impetuous, passionate, unpredictable. Her hair was the color of burnished copper. Her eyes, the gray of the sea just before a storm. Each morning, Annie dressed Sylvie in a well-washed, simple smock, smoothed her hair into plaits, and sent her off to school. Neither the plaits nor the girl who wore them tolerated boundaries. If the teacher's was distracted for merely a moment, Sylvie slipped out the schoolhouse door and escaped to freedom. Her flaming hair, released from its bands, fell to her shoulders, blowing across her face. Her piercing blue eyes, looking out between these strands of fire, reflected a restless soul.

Sylvie ran to forest or to river, alone or with someone whom she had enticed to follow. They would leap from river rock to river rock and collect stones, shiny and colorful with the caress of the waters. Sometimes, the children would gather wildflowers and stick them in their hair or clamber up a tree and steal eggs from a bird's nest. One time, when Sylvie was eight, she stripped to her pantalettes and swam downstream like a small fish, her red hair cascading out upon the river.

Her father, alerted by the school, cut a green shoot and searched the water's edge until he came upon the girls. He chased Sylvie and chastised her until blood spotted her legs.

After that, there was no more school. Sylvie was eight now, old enough to help with her two baby brothers and learn to sew and cook. The people in town called her a devil child and turned their heads when she passed by. She was the moral in bedtime stories, and the insinuation in the preacher's Sunday sermons.

Once a circle of boys tormented her, throwing stones and names. Sylvie leapt upon them like a demon spirit, screaming, clawing, biting until they dropped their rocks and fled.

Life passed by, and the town thought of other things. The strange became familiar with time. When her duties were done and the sun sunk low in the sky, Sylvie disappeared from home. She wandered the woods, the river, the fields, and other lonely places, her imagination, her only friend.

It was August 31st, the hottest day of the year. Sylvie was almost eleven now, grown to take responsibility in the house and on the farm. The heat this summer had turned Pine Ridgesere and brown.Farmers clustered in the feed store and mourned their crops. Somewhere, round midnight, a spark from a forgotten ember traced a glowing circle in thehearth of the Calhoun house. It grew to a flame and then to a conflagration. Peter was safe, across the river, with his new wife. Hank, Annie, Sylvie and the two babies slept. Sylvia was awakened first. She could see flames licking around her door and smoke curling in beneath the jamb. Panicked, she leapt from her bed and ran to her parents'room: "Escape! Escape!" Dodging the pursuing tongues of fire, they fled toward the outside. Annie cried for her babies, screaming in the loft, but Hank held her back, "It's too late, too late, there's nothing to be done." As if God or the Devil himself was protecting her, Sylvie re-entered the collapsing house and pulled her brothers from their beds, carrying, dragging them to safety. The house was gone. The family was whole.

There was no recovery from the disaster. Everything the family had was gone. An evil aura hung over the land. The family was scarred, not so much in body, but in mind. Some said Sylvie was to blame, making spells in the dark.

I was born the night of the fire.

Hank, the boys, and his wife went to live with a cousin in an adjoining town. Sylvie refused to follow. With his wife not yet recovered from childbirth and a new baby in need of attention, my father was glad to welcome Sylvie into his home.

She became my second mother, my protector, my friend. I never knew life without her. I ran to her with my first steps. I cuddled in her arms when the mares of the night galloped through my dreams. We walked along the paths in the woods and watched the sun glint on the river rocks. She told me stories of sprites and spirits. On Sunday, when Sylvie dressed in a long, satin skirt for church, she would let me slide down her knees to the floor. Then we would both collapse, laughing.

Sylvie made a garden in back of our house. Together we planted tomatoes, onions, lettuce, and beans. A special section of the garden was allotted to herbs, some familiar and others gathered from the woods. The plants thrived under her watchful touch.

My mother, a plain-spoken, practical woman, didn't quite trust Sylvie. She had heard the tales and was fearful that I might go the same way. But Peter, my brother, remembered his brothers and insisted that if Sylvie left, he would leave too.

Everything changed one morning in the spring of 1875. Sylvie was 18 and I was 8. She had grown beautiful. Her hair was a glowing mane of red, tied back with a ribbon and curling about her face. Some days her eyes flashed sapphire blue, others, they held a touch of gray like an incoming storm. Her skin remained creamy with a sprinkle of freckles across her nose even when the sun browned the rest of us.

We all expected young men in town to come calling, but they didn't. They sensed a touch of wildness still there, and they were afraid. My mother worried Sylvie would be alone all her life. "Watch that you don't become like her," she told me. "Fit in with the world, don't run from it."

That spring morning, a stranger rode up to our door on a brown roan. He asked for a drink of water and directions. Sylvie gave him both. He was a black-haired Irishman with blue eyes that rivaled Sylvie's in intensity, a broad smile and an infectious laugh. He loved Sylvie from the first moment he saw her. She loved him too, as if she had been struck by lightning.

He told us he traveled many weeks all the way from California and he and his horse were exhausted. My father offered to let him bide a while among us. In the evenings when the fire flickered across the hearth, he told us stories. He talked about the Indians and the railroad that stretched clear across the country, the mountains of California higher and drier than ours, and how he had struck a vein of silver and become rich. We sat with our mouths agape to hear about worlds so different from ours in Pine Ridge.

For three months, Fallon O'Neill, that was his name, stayed in the bedroom across from the kitchen. He would help Sylvie milk the cow and sit on the lawn beside the garden while she tended the plants. Often they'd sneak off to the woods and feast on tiny, spring strawberries or gather watercress for salads. I was fascinated at first, but I became jealous. Sylvie no longer belonged just to me.

The flush on her cheeks got the housewives talking. An Irishman had planted a seed in a Virginia girl. That's what they said, but it wasn't true. He could have. She would have let him. But he didn't. He did buy her a blue dress all the way from New York that made her eyes shine, and he gave her bits and pieces of silver jewelry crafted by Indians, or so he claimed. When she wore her finery, I thought she looked like a magical, fairy princess. I felt honored to have her living in our house.

My father and Fallon proposed business together. They sat for hours in the study. Their plans were not shared with the women, though my father trusted him like a brother. My mother shook her head. "This is all going to come to no good," she said.

One day, Fallon announced he must leave to conduct business far away. We were all sad, even me who was secretly glad to have Sylvie to myself again. Sylvie cried the hardest. Her heart could not bear to see him go.

"I'll be back," he promised. "Look for me on the first day of spring, round midnight."

Sylvie believed him with a faith built on love. Each March 20th , she would put on her blue dress, and from sundown to sunup, she'd stand by the window overlooking the road.

Five years passed and he never came. Sylvie put away her clothes of color and dressed in mourning black. She ate little. Her eyes became pools of loneliness.

She became famous for her herbs. When someone was sick, and the doctor only shook his head, they came for Sylvie. They knew her ministrations were inspired by black magic, but they were desperate to live. I was thirteen now and had my friends and my studies. Sometimes I would follow her to a sickroom and marvel at her gentleness and knowledge. For the most part, however, we were no longer so close. The difference between thirteen and twenty-three was a chasm.

Rumor had it that an Irishman with wild eyes and black hair was robbing banks all up and down the Carolinas and into Virginia. He would gallop into town on his fiery horse, brandishing a silver pistol. Five minutes and he was gone with collateral and savings from the nearest bank. A month later, he would strike again.

Some said it was Fallon and they looked at Sylvie as if she were his co-conspirator. My father and my mother said Irishmen were as common as bees in honey these days. It could be anyone. But I wasn't so sure.

The morning of March 20, 1880 was grey. By noon, the winds were whipping whitecaps in the river. Birds shrieked, flying from tree to tree in a fever of anxiety. Our cow lowed in her stall, kicking at the wooden slats. A general uneasiness filled the air. As the day progressed, the clouds grew larger and blacker. By evening, the wind was whipping the trees, bending their heads to the ground. Rain came with a force never seen before, falling in sheets, filling the river, and hammering the roof. Deliberately, the river climbed out of its banks and clawed its way to our back porch. Strangely, in all of this, there were times of quiet. The noise would abate, and, except for the yellowish cast in the air, everything was normal. Then the intensity would build again. Now the river made its way around the corner of the house, submerging the flower beds and sneaking into the barn.

31

My mother and father took me and sought refuge in the hurricane cellar. Sylvie wouldn't go. It was the first day of spring and she was dressing for her annual watch of the road on the chance Fallon would return at last. The hours passed. The river's fingers reached our front steps, and the wind roared.

Round midnight, I couldn't keep myself back any longer. I pulled away from my parents, ran up the wooden steps, and lifted the trap door. I saw Sylvie running down the stairs, hair flying behind her as if each scarlet tendril had a will of its own. Her face was white; her body shaking. My father's hand grabbed me, pulling me back underground. Before the trapdoor closed over my head, I heard the sound of hooves, the rumble of wagon wheels, and a cry in the wind, "Sylvie....!" Suddenly, the great willow crashed against our roof and someone screamed.

They never found her. My mother said the river had taken back its own, swallowing Sylvie's body and burying her in mud and debris. No one heard the wagon but me. My father said it was the shrieking of the wind that called her name. But, in my mind, I believe, as God is in his heaven, Sylvie is safe and finally in her beloved's arms.

Judith Diamond: For most of my life, I've been a teacher and a writer. Presently, I am teaching digital literacy, math, and English to adults. I have published a variety of books and articles from books on Laos and the Solomon Islands in a series called Enchantment of the World, to a workbook on mathematics and an article in a Japanese magazine about an American singer. Greece has a special place in my heart as I was married for many years to an immigrant from Tripolis and have five children who all look like their father. I live and work in the USA, near Chicago, Illinois where I spin stories, make gardens, and find new places on my bicycle or by riding high up on the EL, the maze of train cars that takes traveler to every nook of the city.

One Shot
David Butler

The pub was heaving with the rugby crowd. Above the din and jostling, Vikram suggested Chez Max.Pyotr guffawed:'Yeah, after JJ's round!'JJ had a bit of a name. My funds were running low, but I'd no wish to head back to the flat. So I told them I'd nip out to the nearest ATM. Behind Janine's back, Vikram made an obscene gesture.

It was dark outside, the neon dark of the city. It must've been raining to judge from the glare off the asphalt and hiss of taxis. It felt cold after the fug inside. I shivered. I hadn't brought my jacket. Besides the usual smokers there were few about; no-one at all at the ATM. No queue. There was a figure cocooned in a sleeping-bag. Hoody; face turned away. You don't normally notice these guys. But there was something about him made me look twice. The hood was up, the head angled so that onlya beard protruded. Something made me hunker down, all the same. Once I'd stowed the cash away.

His face was gaunt. And yellowed, even allowing for the street neon. The protuberant eyes refused to meet mine. A jolt took me, and I clicked my fingers:'Donal Reid! For God's sake...'The eyes flitted onto mine, then rolled away as though having difficulty focusing. 'It's me. Podge.' I ran my palms over my baldness, as though to make a joke of the years. 'Paddy McHale.'

No response, not even a flicker. Temporarily, I doubted. I was cold in my shirtsleeves. There was, besides, a busy-body footering at the ATM, watching. So I ran through my wallet for anything smaller than a twenty, to gloss over the awkward situation. I located a fiver and held it out.

'You can keep your fiver,' he said.

I hadn't seen Donal Reid in twenty years. None of us had. He'd disappeared when I was in university. Left without trace.

His name had come up the previous September at the school reunion, that was the size of it. There was a rumour that put him in Boston, another in a doss-house in London. Someone had even heard he'd died. Any queries about Donnie tended to be directed toward me; for a couple of years in school, we'd been next to inseparable.

It had been one of those intense friendships between adolescents. He was a year older, painfully quiet, tall, bit of a loner. Except, that is, where it came to rugby. What he lacked in bulk he made up for in instinct. He was part of the team that was just pipped by Rock in the Senior Cup final. But he was never one for the repartee that's part and parcel of that sport and, inside Dublin's business fraternity, long outlives it. Donnie would far sooner slip away once a match was done. Only for that, he might well have captained the side.

I was bloody useless when it came to sports. I was pudgy, and to make up for it, a class joker. I was a good nine inches shorter than Donnie, so we must've struck classmates and teachers alike as quite the comical pairing. For two years though, as my late mother always put it, we'd lived in one another's pockets. What it was we found to talk about into or through the night, and with such intensity, I can scarcely imagine. If my reasoning could usually get the better of his, he burned with such sudden ardour that my common-sense felt dull next to it.

The friendship burned out, or fell away. I went to college, took a degree. He went to ground, to follow some vague dream of being a writer. He'd won some poetry contest or other, or he'd a contact who was a literary agent, or perhaps both. I'd be more confident of the details if it wasn't for a row that finished off the waning friendship. The occasion was my eighteenth; the location, the function room of the Mont Clare off Merrion Square.

I should've mentioned, Donnie was adopted. His foster parents were about two decades older than mine. An only child, too, which as my mother used say, explained a lot. Perhaps that was why he could decide with so little compunction to abandon the nest. One way or another, he'd got it into his head that I should go with him. That was the import of his diatribe as he button-holed me, coming out of the jacks.

'What in God's name would I do in London? Solve maths theorems? With respect Donnie it's different for you.'

'With respect McHale you're talking shite. What you'd do is live! You're supposed to know about life at eighteen years of age? What I'm proposing, we take life by the scruff of the neck. At our age, Rimbaud had all his best work written.'

'Rimbaud,' I muttered. All I wished at that moment was that none of my new crowd would chance upon us.

'You're doing what, accounting?' I shrugged, yeah. 'At eighteen years of age, you've decided to spend your life to adding up other people's sums. Come off it Podge! Is that what you were given life for?' He shook me, only half playful. 'One shot, remember?'His eyes were huge, and, I noticed, veined. One shot was the one thing he ever said on the rugby pitch, a rallying-cryfor his team-mates. They'd even nicknamed him One-shot.

At this point, a girl heading into the toilet threw me a sympathetic grimace. Most of my college friends thought Donal Reid faintly ludicrous.A few insisted he was a junkie. Yet something held me, like the wedding guest in the poem. 'What about your folks, Donnie?' He smirked. 'You have told them, right?'

'That's a cop out!' He nodded, slowly. I could guess what was coming. 'Let me ask you something...'

'When I'm on my deathbed,' I supplied. It had been another of his catch-cries.

'When you're on your death-bed, and you look back on a life spent adding up figures, how are you going to feel? Proud of yourself? Ok. Suppose you make it. You get a house. Your kids go to Belvedere College. Is that all there is, Podge?'

'You tell me, Don.'

'I thought that, I'd hang myself. Swear to God I would. What d'you say, Podge? Give it a year. It doesn't work out, go back to your degree. Please!' Here he was actually tugging at my sleeve. 'Come with me.'

'Not everyone can be an idealist, Donnie.'

'That's bullshit. It's not about being anything. It's about not being a..., a coward.'

I released my arm from his. 'My mother's not well.'

'Don't pass the buck! Jesus Christ, I'm asking you to...'

But I'd already begun upstairs.

'Fuck sake, Podge... '

I hurried through the doors. To my intense discomfort I'd realised he was crying.

Six months later he disappeared. It even made the newspapers. His shoes and parka had been found by Portobello Bridge, but nobody was ever pulled from the canal. For several weeks his face looked out from photos pasted to lampposts and bus shelters. Over time these faded, like so many leaves. Why he'd left in so startling a manner I never learned. Perhaps he'd run up a debt, or had got involved with someone. I only hoped that, from whatever garret he'd holed up in, he'd at least written his foster parents.

I told a lie just now. I said none of us had heard a word about him in twenty years. In fact, at the ten year reunion, Mixer Murphy, the last of the Jesuits, had brought along a slim volume of poetry. A chapbook, published by an obscure London Press.H, by Donal Reid. It had been sent to the school: no letter, no note, not even signed. Mixer pressed it on me, insisted I take it. I let on to be delighted, leafed through it on the night bus, and never once thought of it afterwards. I never got poetry.

A few catcalls brought me back to the present. The office party was grouped outside the pub, variously gesticulating and whistling. Janine, with whom I'd had an ill-advised fling, began to approach, dangling my jacket from a finger. I immediately rose and took a few steps towards her. 'Who's your pal?' Her smirk, and her boozy breath, and the whole smug set of them filled me with sudden loathing. I tugged the jacket from her - she was letting on to resist - and turned away. 'Well fuck you,' she said. I listened to her heels clack away, then returned to the cowled figure. 'Come on Donal. I'll get you something to eat.'

It took a good ten minutes to cajole him. At first he simply ignored my entreaties. Then for a while he got hostile. At last he stood, teetered, said 'If it makes you feel better about yourself,'and shambled towards a fast food joint. Looking at the state of him, we'd little hope of getting in anywhere else.

The light was glaringly white, and under it, the ravages were shocking. His head was little more than a skull papered over with mottled skin. This was overwhelmingly yellow; yellowed, too, the globes of his eyes. The beard was a sad excuse, though it lent his mien something of the medieval ascetic. Worst of all was the ruin when he opened his mouth. Seeing my revulsion, he grinned. 'Methadone, baby. That's the smile she gives you.'

Mostly he sat in antagonistic silence. His manner of tearing at the kebab was ugly, deliberately so. He had considerable difficulty swallowing. He refused entirely to answer anything pertaining to his past. Neither would he talk about his foster parents, nor say whether they lived. At one point I noticed his habit of glancing at my wedding band, which I'd been twiddling. I covered it apologetically. 'You're married,' he stated rather than asked, mouth full. 'Thather with your jacket?' For a second I was lost. Then I recalled Janine, her sardonic walk, her severe lipstick. 'God, no!' Was there mockery in his dirty eyes?

'Kids?'

I shook my head.

'Happy, are you?'

'Are you?' The retort was instant. I'd no great wish to think about Leanne, much less talk to this stranger about her. Time enough for all that. Then the kebab, half-eaten, dropped to the table and he dry-retched. I clocked the staff severely watching us. 'Hey,' I said, happily lighting on a topicas I helped him stand, 'I came across a book of yours. Mixer gave it to me. Mixer Murphy? Yeah, so he passed it on to me, oh a good ten years now it must be. Book of poetry it was.'

For the first time, something approximating interest animated his face. Something approaching the school-friend of old. 'What did you think of it?' he squinted.

'God, Donnie, it's been a long time, you know?'

He snorted, tossed his head. At the door I let on I had to head off in the opposite direction. 'McHale, for Christ's sake lend me a hundred,' he said.

I'd fobbed him off with forty, muttering we were months behind on the mortgage. It was no lie, we were behind. I watched his figure lope off towards the canal. Then I began to drift in the direction of Spenser Dock. My steps were reluctant, my insides jittery. God alone knows what cocktail of thoughts, of emotions, of memories the encounter had churned up. I'd been a prey to mood-swings of late, and that was a part of it, too.

I recalled what my father once said. For everyone that achieves their dream, there's ninety-nine with real talent who don't. The ninety-nine that spend their lives not quite making the cut: in golf; or in tennis. The ninety-nine that don't quite win the award, or get the audition. All very well to be romantic about it, Podge. Remember, a paternal finger went up, biographies are only ever written about the one percent who made it.

He needn't have been concerned. I'd no great talent, nor ambition. He should have saved that sermon for Donal Reid. But no doubt he'd have replied (the young Donnie, the Donnie I'd hung around with, the Donnie who made the great plays on the rugby pitch) that at least the ninety-nine could rest easy on their death-beds. They'd given it their all. You see Mr McHale, you've only the one shot at life.

Having no wish to entertain his 'happy are you?',I wondered if I still had that poetry volume; whether, if I had,I could lay my hand on it.H. Like rugby posts. I had an urge to decipher the observations he'd collected ten years before, if that's what they were. Before he became a full-on junkie, if that's what he was. Methadone, baby. For the life of me I couldn't remember unpacking it after the move to Spenser Dock. Once or twice, in school, Donnie had shown me a poem he'd composed, but he'd always had to explain it.

By the time I got to the river my thoughts had returned to the flat. Leanne would be asleep, or pretending to be. The marriage had long since cooled off. To be fair to her, she had taken her one shot. This was before we'd met. For several years after college she'd tried to knock a living out of interior design. These days, when she could get it, she worked in HR. Probably we'd have gone our separate ways, in another world. But we'd bought the place at the peak. Besides, if she were to finally decide on a kid, time was running against her.

Out of the blue, I was seized by the unfairness of it all. Why hadn't things worked out for her? When had my enthusiasm waned? After all, she was still a fine looking woman. Ours was still an enviable address. I looked at the figure looking back from the merciless elevator mirror. Five foot eight, balding, thumbprints pushed under each sardonic eye. What if I could have seen that character, that night in the Mont Clare? Mother always said you play the hand you're dealt. But had I played it? Then I saw again the skeletal figure shambling away towards Baggot St Bridge. A single, slender volume seemed scant reward for a life thrown away.

Inside the flat I was more careful than usual. Solicitous. Leanne's bare shoulder was above the duvet. I folded my clothes onto a chair and drew myself in against her bed-warm body. I held her close, my face tickled by her hair. She muttered something. Then all at once I was sobbing, deep, painful sobs: for the world; for Leanne Kearney; for lost youth. For the way that enthusiasm, or love, evaporates.

I pulled closer, kissed the nape of her neck. 'You're drunk,' she said.

Memories always start around midnight
Suzanne Elvidge

I couldn't stop looking at her. She was smiling, a small secret smile. A smile that reminded me of a purring cat. She would people-watch for a moment or two and then scribble furiously in her notebook. She reached absently for the pint glass with a pale, ringless hand, and downed the last mouthful. She took a cigarette from the open packet in front of her, tapping it on the table and lighting it with her hands cupped carefully around the battered steel lighter. Shielding the yellow-blue flame from non-existent draughts.

I couldn't believe my luck. Here I was in my favourite bar, the straightest environment I knew, waiting for the jazz to begin, and there was this beautiful woman looking at me. Just the thought of her made me smile, ran shivers up and down my spine. Made me want to play my fingers over her skin, share smoky, blurred kisses, whisper pointless, pretty rubbish in her ears, rub out the worried frown line between her eyes. Nibble that beautiful, nameless place just at the edge of her lower lip. Push my hands into her cropped, glossy black-brown hair and pull her red-painted lips up to meet mine.

As she breathed out her first lungful into the smokiness of the bar, she saw me looking at her. Her smile spread slowly wider, crinkling around her eyes, still secret, still amused but welcoming me in. I felt myself flush, looked down at the half-eaten meal in front of me, and fumbled with my book. I hadn't wanted to attract her attention, had just wanted to watch her.

And then she looked away, and I thought I must have made a mistake. It happens. No one wears a label that says 'I like women' where I hang out. Though I admit it would make life a bit easier. Gay bars would make this game even simpler, but I hate gay bars. I am so not scene I'm almost coming at it from the other side. I wandered into one by accident once and thought I was back in college, the desperation for a shag hung so heavy in the air. So I drink beer in pubs, watch people, listen to jazz and write. And seemingly get looked at by beautiful women. She was so my type. Boyish, lean, with dark urchin cut hair. Skin with a touch of olive. She was dressed in a deep blue shift dress, and had an end of a long day weary look. There was a half-eaten meal and an empty glass on her table.

She was dressed in black. A snug fitting, black T shirt over small breasts and a lean body. Skinny black jeans and battered brown suede boots with high, solid heels. Long legs stretched out under the table. Her hair was strawberry blonde, tousled and curling to her shoulders. She had pale skin and wore little make up. Sooty dark mascara round startlingly blue eyes, and terracotta-brown lipstick. She raised her left hand to me in acknowledgement.

I caught her eyes and we locked gaze for a heart-stopping moment. She looked down as if someone had slapped her. I had caught her looking. I finished a page and reached for my pint glass. It was empty. I needed another drink.

I felt like I'd been seen doing something I shouldn't. But I had to look back. She looked amused, her smile one of those that goes down rather than up, and tipped her empty glass towards me, raising her arched, dark eyebrows in query. I realised she was asking me if I wanted a drink. I shook my head, and she walked towards the bar.

At the bar, Adam handed me a gin and tonic, on the house. "Her name's Charlotte, and she's staying here for a couple of nights on business. She's been bawled out by her boss. Be kind to her."

The barman must have told her what I was drinking, because as she walked back she put a gin and tonic on the scarred pub table. Saying not a word, she went back to her scribbling and people-watching. What was I supposed to do? I couldn't pretend that it hadn't happened, but I didn't want to get involved, not here, not now, and not with a woman. I just couldn't help looking at her. She shook out a cigarette, looked at me, and smiled that slow, sweet smile that was directed as much inward as outward.

Today had been complicated enough. The deal had fallen through because I'd been given the wrong information, and then James had called me, shrieking that I 'should have known' that the figures were out. Using my well-known psychic powers and the 24 hours I'd had to prepare for the trip because he couldn't be bothered to go.

She picked up her notebook and scarred biker's jacket and stood up, and I felt a surge of relief and a stab of regret. I wanted to know her, and somewhere deep inside me I wanted to touch her.

"I'm Samantha. Sam." She looked so freaked out that I instantly regretted it, but had to follow through. "I'm just going through to hear the jazz. It's 'Club Class' tonight, and the music is very mellow. And it fills up quickly, so if we want a table we'd better go through now."

She said that she ought to go. It had been a long day, and she didn't have any cash on her. Her voice was low, quiet. She looked down at the table, studying the surface so intensely it was as if she was memorising it for a test.

"You're a resident, you'll get in for free. And you might as well finish your drink. It was from Adam at the bar. He's a nice boy, not quite my type if you know what I mean, but I've known him for years." Hearing that the drink was from Adam somehow soothed her, and I felt a wince of sadness. I must have read all the signals so wrong.

I noticed a brief flash of hurt and couldn't work out what I'd done. I stuck out my hand automatically and we shook hands formally. I then realised that I didn't want to let go. We held hands for a moment, or an hour, I wasn't sure which, but it was certainly longer than courtesy required. Whatever, the flash of hurt was replaced by a warm smile.

"I might as well, I guess. I'm only going to end up sitting in my room, otherwise. I'm Charlotte." I picked up my drink and followed Sam through to the small basement room where the jazz group was setting up. Five middle-aged guys from Sheffield, but when they started playing Thelonious Monk's Round Midnight we could have been in a New York jazz dive. When the music stopped I turned to Sam and asked her if she wanted a drink. "This one's on expenses. I need to get something out of today."

Charlotte came back with a pint of beer for me, a gin and tonic for her and pork scratchings, peanuts and crisps. She told me that she hadn't known what I wanted, but that she felt kind of peckish, as she really hadn't fancied supper. So she bought a bit of everything. I smiled and ripped open the pack of pork scratchings. I looked around the wood-panelled basement room. The tables were lit by candles in Jack Daniels square optic bottles, the upside-down labels dripping with wax. The ceiling was nicotine-yellow, stained and wounded by time and subsidence. Outside life moved on above head height, unnoticed.

"How good does life get. Jazz, beer, deep fried fatty leftovers and good company" She looked at me quizzically, and then smiled, the first genuine one of the night.

The music started up again, this time with a guest vocalist. She was tiny and childlike, but with a voice that belied her size and age. The music was loud and sexy; she belted out jazz standards with a husky hitch to her voice, a breathy darkness as sticky as treacle. The music made me melt, made the stresses of the day disappear.

"Can I beg a cigarette?" Sam was obviously in deep and my voice made her jump. "Sorry, I didn't mean to startle you. You were miles away." Her secret smile was directed at the pretty singer, who seemed to be singing directly back, and I felt an unexpected stab of jealousy. "I really shouldn't, but gin isn't quite the same without one."

Charlotte smiled, guiltily biting her bottom lip between her teeth. I had been miles away. Bess had the sexiest voice. We had a bit of a history. Not much of one; I had thought I was falling in love with her one long, hot, drowsy summer, but she think the same. We had settled into a flirty friendship and she was singing 'That old Devil called Love' right into my insides, warming me through and making my skin tingle.

"I'll get some from the bar. Adam owes me a pack anyway. I'll pick up another drink while I'm there. Gin again?" I brushed off her protestations.

I watched her as she walked to the bar. She had a confident step, and an easy familiarity with everyone in the small audience. She sat back down with the drinks and the cigarettes, giggling at something Adam had said to her.

"He seems nice. The lad at the bar. He was really kind to me earlier on when I got that rotten call from my boss," I whispered. Sam looked... well, I don't know... almost jealous. We were sending wildly mixed signals to each other, and I wasn't quite sure what to do.

"I've known Adam for years. We went to school together, and just before I went away to college we had a bit of a fling. No offence to him, but it was that experience that convinced me I was gay," I whispered back, my breath just disturbing the short dark hair cut neatly round her ears. I watched her carefully, to see how she reacted. Would there be interest? Disgust? Nope, just a little, inscrutable smile.

I peeled the cellophane off the packet of cigarettes, scrunched it up and tucked it neatly in my pocket. I've always hated people putting cigarette wrappings into ashtrays. Probably part of the same urge that makes me fold crisp packets into neat little triangles. I pulled out the foil and eased two cigarettes up. She tugged one out with a pearl pink, perfectly oval nail. Mine are kept filed square and short because otherwise they catch random keys on the keyboard (and my typing is bad enough as is), but hers looked manicured and pampered. She ran her other hand through her dark hair, and I leaned forward and lit her cigarette for her with my old steel American lighter. The flame briefly reflected in her dark brown eyes. She pulled on the cigarette like a woman thirsty, leaning back in her chair and blowing the smoke straight up in the air. She laughed for the first time that night, welling up from deep inside, and relaxed into the sexy, earthy music. The harsh lines between her eyes drifted away.

A few couples, mostly older, got up to dance, and I itched to feel her in my arms, but I thought that would be too much, too far, too fast. As the music stopped we slipped into an easy companionship, talking, listening, laughing, maybe even flirting a little. We both reached for Adam's cigarettes at the same time, and there was a shiver of electricity – for me, anyway. I couldn't really tell for her. And on some level it didn't matter. On another level; well, it was driving me crazy.

She made me laugh. And after a day like I'd had, well, that was a big thing. Someone had put one of Bess' CDs on, and this provided a mellow but slightly charged undertone to everything we said. It filled any gaps in the conversation, but to be honest there weren't very many of those. We'd got to the point where we'd talked about everything and nothing, and felt like we'd known each other for years. I guess that the gin, beer and cigarettes helped, but I didn't really care. I was relaxed and laughing for what seemed like the first time in forever, or at least since the last time I'd been out with friends. And I thought they would like Sam. Somehow that was important.

Everything had got so stressful of late. Work was on top of me – though I loved every minute of it, some of the hours were pretty bad – and my social life had just dissolved under it. It was so good just to let go, to talk about something that didn't involve business consultancy. We'd read some of the same books and seen some of the same films. We argued over politics (one of those alcohol-fuelled arguments where it's only halfway through that you realise that you are both talking from the same perspective). And then all of a sudden it was last orders. Bess and the group came back on for one more song. It was 'That Old Devil called Love' again and I desperately wanted to dance. But my mouth just couldn't ask. Instead, I laid my hand on hers. It was around midnight.

"I've got a rather nice bottle of whisky up in my room, given to me by a client. Do you want one for the road?"

I'm sorry, was that me talking? If it wasn't, I have no clue where that came from. And if it was, I still don't.

I think she's just asked me up to her room for a drink. I assumed nothing, though Adam gave me his patented 'get your coat, you've pulled' look, and I stuck my tongue out at him as we walked to the resident's stairs. And then, somehow, I'm holding her, getting the smoke-blurred kisses that I've been dreaming of all night. The chance to taste her tongue, her lips, her skin. Her perfume was medicinal in my mouth, and afterwards I saw my lipstick stark on her pale neck like a bruise. She looked at me dazed, and I worried that I had pushed things too far, too fast. But then she smiled, a dazzling, sweet smile that lit up the face I had first seen drawn and stressed, and pulled me down to her. I ran my hands through her soft, scented, smoke-drifted hair. I felt her alive under my fingers and mouth. I knew that this may be all I get, that she might just be straight and curious, but I also felt that there might be a connection. I decided to just wait and see.

Suzanne Elvidge: I am a freelance medical and healthcare writer based in the beautiful Peak District in the UK. I have written since my hand could clutch a pencil and my work allows me to combine my two loves – science and words. Outside of science, I write short stories and monologues. I had short stories published in the Bitch Lit and Read by Dawn anthologies, and in magazines.

Huggas
Mark Perfect

Ever felt better after you've done a good deed for someone else? Most people do. Do you wonder why?

This is a story about Huggas. Each person has their own Hugga. Embra, one such Hugga, lived, as most Huggas do, in a bedroom. George's bedroom. He had fiery orange, iridescent hair that stood up sharply in spikes almost half his height. It was all the more striking, because he was only about the size of a mouse.

One Friday night, in the sock draw of George's bedroom wardrobe, Embra relaxed, listening to music on his headphones, nodding away to the beat. His hair pulsed with blue light to the rhythm, as it always did. Later, he climbed up the side of the sock draw, and slid snuggly into his, or rather George's sock, that he had positioned, hanging like a Christmas stocking. His nose just peeped over the top of the sock. As his head slowly and slightly tilted to the left, a brrrrr, chrrrr, brrrrr emanated from his nose and he drifted off to sleep. He'd had a peaceful night because George had, had a busy day a school and then come home to do lots of homework. George hadn't had time help anyone during the day so Embra was not hugging tonight.

The next day, being a Saturday, was much more eventful for Embra. George had been helping his Dad, Roasti design a car in the morning. That was Roasti's job. George never appeared overly active in helping his Dad, but Roasti liked to get George's input on certain aspects of the design. George was quite content just watching his Dad at work anyway, almost hypnotised at times, as his pencil caressed curves on the car's silhouette. In the afternoon, he had been helping his Mum, Jetti, plant a new palm tree in a sunny spot in the back garden. She was a part-time gardener. Suffice to say, George had been helping others a lot today. So he would be rewarded later with a hug from Embra. That night, as George drifted off into a deep, well earnt sleep, Embra, slowly pushed open the sock draw and clambered silently down the sheer face of the wardrobe. He ran across the soft, deep, bronze carpet to George's bed. He jumped up and clung onto the overhanging duvet on the right-hand side of George and clambered up and across towards him. Silently lifting the duvet up a jar, he edged onto George's left shoulder and gave George the slightest tug towards him, then settled to sleep there for the night. George's left leg twitched almost like a switch being turned on.

Parents understandably, are more demanding on their Hugga's than their children. An enormous proportion of a parent's day is spent doing things for their children, not themselves. So it's inevitable that each parent's Hugga will be harder at work than a child's. Not only that, but parents' Huggas are older, the same age as their recipients, with diminishing hug reserves. So when Jetti began helping at a homeless shelter, her Hugga, Enclo, quickly became exhausted. Jetti, of course, began to lose her jovial demeanour after a few weeks, deprived of theincreased quality of hug she required. Which, given how much selfless work she was doing, wasn't just. Embra was in a quandary. Should he help Enclo? He wasn't sure if he had the hug reserves to cope with Jetti's and George's requirements. He knew Cuddlo, Roasti's Hugga, was too old to help. So, as there seemed no other option, he decided he'd try to reward them both.

To Embra's surprise, he found he could cope with demands of Jetti and George, with no side-effects himself. A couple of weeks in, he decided to ditch his evening's music listening, and try out some car drawings, for a change. It was hard not be inspired by Roasti. George proudly hung many of his Dad's drawings on his bedroom wall, which often distracted Embra en route to George for a hug. He sometimes just stood there gawping at them, before remembering his task. Embra wasn't a natural at drawing, but, because he had to use glow in the dark pencils, inside the sock drawer, it was pretty good fun. A nice change too. That night he coped with Jetti's and George's hug needs, but only just. He thought perhaps he was just having an off day. He didn't draw again for a week. The night that followed another drawing session, Embra noticed again, that he was only just coping with Jetti and George's needs. This time, he realised the only thing he had been doing differently was drawing, instead of listening to music. As he pondered this, he concluded that he'd draw for a few evenings in succession and see what happened. Sure enough, after each night, he progressively felt more and more tired, as his hug reserves got smaller and smaller. On the third night he couldn't fully reward George, because Jetti had exhausted his reserves. As soon as Embra reintroduced listening to music the following evening, everything was back to normal. Embra embarked upon some "research". He crept into George's parents' bedroom, and after a lot of searching, found Roasti's Hugga, Cuddlo reading under DIY mini lamplight in a wall cavity. He was pleased to have eventually found him, but frustrated, because somehow he needed to see another Hugga listening to music. He had a hunch. Cuddlo had to be the focus of the "research" because Enclo didn't enjoy listening to music.

After weeks of fruitless "research trips", he finally observed Cuddlo listening to some Latin music, of some sort. The problem was, Embra hadn't predicted the inevitable. His hair started pulsing with blue light, to the rhythm of the music. In the dark, his hair was like a slow-motion, upward scrolling beacon of lightning. Suffice to say, it was quite noticeable, and even though Embra was only peaking on Cuddlo through atiny gap in the wall cavity "door", Cuddlo was dazzled. After a few seconds Cuddlo came to his senses, and hurried Embra into the wall cavity, where he lived. Although none of the human family were around, he didn't want Embra to be seen, and he was definitely eye-catching! Embra sat himself on a small loose block of wall plaster, while Cuddlo remained standing, still in semi-shock. Embra himself, was still trying to take it all in, but he managed to explain to Cuddlo that he was obtaining extra hug reserves by listening to music. And that he'd stumbled across this, by drawing one night, instead of listening to music. He didn't know how, but the pulsing blue light in his hair seemed to act like a charging indicator light on an electronic gadget. Embra just thought all Huggas' hair did this when they listened to music. Huggas were quite solitary creatures, and he'd never listened to any music with another Hugga present, so never thought twice about his hair lighting up. Cuddlo's certainly didn't.

There was a gentle tapping on the wall next to where Embra was sitting. Enclo had heard all the commotion and wanted to know what was going on. After explaining, Embra and Cuddlo tested Enclo's hair for lights, with some more of Cuddlo's music, but there were none. In all their years, Cuddlo and Enclo had never seen or heard of anything like it. Embra had a very unusual and valuable gift. Enclo enveloped Embra in a heartfelt hug, that took Embra by surprise. He'd never received a hug before. Enclo explained that she was so proud of him. Not for succeeding in helping Jetti and George at the same time, but for deciding to try to do it. That was what Enclo saw as most important. Initially, Embra didn't feel any different following Enclo's hug, but as they returned to their respective homes, Embra noticed himself smiling for seemingly no reason, and a warmth filled his mind. As Embra drifted off to sleep that night, he realised he probably wouldn't receive any other reward for his extra efforts over the last few weeks or into the future, but somehow the immeasurable reward he'd received felt enough.

Mark Perfect *lives in Devon, UK, near the ocean. Shares a house with his parents, who look after him. Unfortunately, he has some health problems. Writing is his escape. Loves stories with creatures, and trying to find amusing aspects from everyday life. Has a degree in Geography and a Masters degree in Sports Nutrition. Is passionate about sports car design, particularly flowing curves. Has studied sports car design, and designs cars occasionally. Competed in regional standard swimming races, and Grand Prix table tennis events. Enjoys giving and receiving hugs! Hi to everyone, hope you enjoy the story. Go for your dreams.*

Red Beauty or simply Dear
Christina Demertsidou

I saw her through a tram window in Amsterdam. Seeing her there weathered and so lonely, I instantly wanted to know her story. From her condition it was evident that years have passed since she was abandoned. It surprised me that she was not removed by the local authorities. At a neat and such a clean street she looked foreign. She did not belong there. "What's her story?", I asked myself. I am a storyteller but somehow she did not reveal her story to me immediately. That is why even six years later that memory still haunts me. The story was there from the very first sign but I couldn't penn it down just yet. It is certain that she chose me. Her aura pulled my gaze towards her direction. She wanted to be noticed. She wanted to be felt. I was the chosen one and it is my duty to acknowledge her pain. Finally not that long ago, during a two-hour flight I switched my mobile to flight mode and started writing. So here is her story. A story about Red Beauty or simply Dear:

He adored her! She was the very first thing that he wanted to possess badly. He never wanted anything more in his life. From the very first day he saw her, that red beauty, he fell in love. For over a year, he would pass by the store as often as possible to watch her pose at the window as a diva that knows her value. There were other Amsterdam beauties around her but she would stand out. She was unique and she was waiting for him. Over the course of that year, those other beauties were sold. She was stubborn, did not want to give herself to just anyone. She was to be his! She fell in love seeing his eyes, those eyes that admired her, each and every time he visited her. As admiration did not fade away in his eyes, love was born inside her.

The day he came for her, made her feel that their story would be epic. "It can't get any better than this!", she thought each time he cared for her with those enchanted eyes. Together at college, shopping, walks. Her place was always in his bedroom never the garage. That was the cause of so many fights at home, yet she was his and as long as he kept his room clean there was no right for arguing further. Some of his friends would even criticise his choice of colour. He never cared. He had named her 'Dear' while others called their possessions 'babes'. She was not as all the others. She was his 'Dear'.

Nonetheless, no relationships are merry all the time. There were ups and downs. Nothing serious though. Once, she got angry and broke down after a night of confession. He had assured her that she was his one and only. There was no other before her, he said. He lied to her. She hated lies. He said it was nothing serious. Just some baby bicycles he got when he was a child. She was hurt but forgave him as past was past and so there was no reason to worry over that. However, it would have been best if she had walked away back then when another boy wanted to steal her. But, she was loyal to him and would not surrender to anyone else. If only she could think clearly back then. If a man lies once, he will most surely lie again. She was too blind. She trusted him with her life.

"What happened? What changed?", she would often wonder. Well, he never got the guts to tell her. Five years together every day and everything changed once he got work placement away from home. He left her in his bedroom, but she was soon moved to the garage. She did not give up as she trusted that once he is back, she will regain her rightful place. He promised before leaving that he will take her along as soon as possible. "I can't live without you", he said.

He visited a year later. Of course, he called her 'Dear' when he first looked her up, asked how she was doing, and commented that she still was a beauty. Nevertheless, to her surprise he took her for a ride but once returning home he parked her in the garage. "He is tired", she tried to justify him. "Tomorrow things will change", she thought to herself. He stayed for five days. They would go out for rides every day, but he was not speaking to her at all and was always returning her to the garage. He was deep in his thoughts. He was a changed man, it was obvious even from the way he was riding her. He never mentioned of taking her with him, yet she hoped as he had promised!

The night before his departure, he was invited to a friend's house. He locked her to a road sign. The night was long. Drugs, alcohol, girls... He got carried away and at the end did not even remember that she was there waiting for him. A friend dropped him home. He left without saying "bye". He forgot her! He did not even call the Fietsdepot. Reality was cruel. She was abandoned.

Over the years, she saw him drive by the spot he left her. Every time in a different car! Second hand cars, he could afford with his salary. Different colours, different shapes. Things changed when she saw him drive by in a brand new red car. His parents would often speak of getting him such car as a wedding present. Things were obvious. He sure looked up for various cars but never took a year of appreciating one in particular. Two test drives and the choice was made. Not once did he recognise her during those rides. Now it is too late. The damage is fatal. She is irreparable. Yet, she is still waiting for him to come. He hurt her so much, but she still hopes as there is no limit to her faith.

Many more years passed and she was still there, abandoned and forgotten. She was fading away, while her pain was getting deeper and deeper. She had not seen him in years. As time was flying, she was wondering what keeps her alive. Deep inside she knew it was hope. Hope for seeing him again. Hope for redemption. She had so many scenarios for how she wanted her Golgotha to end but she had never imagined what was about to happen.

Around midnight on a rainy day, she first heard a car tyre burst and then saw him seconds before his car crushed her. It was an accident, fate, karma, kismet, or simply how their story was meant to end. Before flying away, he looked at her and his last word was 'Dear'. She was covered in his blood; it was as if she was transformed again into the red beauty she used to be. But, the rain soon washed away his warm blood... He was gone and a thunder shouted a loud 'Dear' that would fade away into three quieter and distant 'Dear'... 'Dear'... 'Dear'... And with the last cry the rain stopped.

No, this was not how she hoped for their story to end. Redemption was meant to heal. No, this was not redemption. He was gone and she was left once more alone. Broken into pieces, and left with nothing to hope for. Yet, she was finally noticed. That same day, she was removed from the street and was placed where she belonged - the Fietsdepot, a place for all bicycles not wanted anymore. She was among 17,000 abandoned bicycles, awaiting her fate. Only a very small proportion of those bicycles were claimed by their owners and she was not one of them. But she was not, as all the others.

Three more months passed, months of meditation. She relived that tragic night over and over again, and had finally come to a conclusion. She used to be 'Dear' to him but he abandoned her. She was forgotten. That night, when he called out 'Dear', he was not referring to her. She was there in front of him but he did not recognise her. She was erased from his memory. She used to be his 'Dear', his very first 'Dear'. Yet, to him 'Dear' were many. By now, she was more than sure that he called 'Dear' his wife too. "What more natural than that?", she thought. He made her feel special as long as she was his 'Dear'. When he erased her from his life, he found another to call 'Dear'. His love made her feel special but his love was ephemeral. That night she was naive, she felt what she needed to feel. He was back and to him she was 'Dear'. However, raw reality and cruel life opened up her eyes. She should have never hoped for redemption. Knowing the truth is what she needed. If only she knew the truth from the very beginning...

Some may say that truth leads to redemption. What she knows now is that truth leaves a scar. A wound heals and pain is gone, but the scar stays with you forever. You will never forget but with truth you can at least live on. She would often wonder about what still keeps her alive, whether it was a new chapter, a second chance to happiness, or maybe a greater purpose. However, she was at Fietsdepot long enough to understand her fate. No-one was coming for her and so she would be either sold for spare parts or shredded into scrap metal. Till one day, everything changed and she could have never predicted such turn of events. A team of volunteers had selected her and hundreds more to be shipped to refugee camps in Greece. She was repaired and loaded into a container. Her journey had just begun. She would be used as a form of transport to help those in so much need. She was a small part of a great project that was an important help for the 50,000 Syrian refugees fleeing Syria's civil war. What she was feeling can't be described by words. Her life had a purpose. She would have a new owner, a new life.

And there he was. She noticed him immediately. He spotted her directly. While others were hurrying to pick just any one, he was slowly walking towards her, examining her. His eyes brought back a feeling buried inside her heart. Those enchanted dark eyes were promising another chance. When he called her 'Azizati', she did not mind. Her new name sounded sweet to her. How surprised she was when she found out that 'Azizati' means 'Dear' in Arabic.

She had an adventurous long life as 'Azizati' and after many years ended back in Amsterdam as part of a street art project. She had become a street decor. Reincarnated into such, she was admired by many. Till one day, an old man stopped to admire her. "You look just like her! Oh 'Dear', where are you?", he cried. He stayed for some time and as if talking to a human he started telling her his story: "When I was a young boy, I had a 'Dear' just like you. She was my one and only. I last saw her during the worst day of my life. Or, so I thought. I was in coma for three months. Maybe it was just a dream..." He looked at her for one more time and walked away.

He was alive! He recognised her that night. She was 'Dear' to him. So this was the truth. So this was redemption. So only time can truly tell...

I hope you liked the story. Seeing that abandoned bicycle inspired me instantly. I felt sorry for it even though it was an inanimate object. I am a person who keeps a first toy somewhere safe as it has a symbolic meaning for me. So what if it is old, broken, ugly... It was my dear toy once and it has to stay safe! I would even try to fix any broken parts so that the toy can function. Yet he, that someone who abandoned the bicycle is a person who forgot his old toy and all the joy he once felt by having it. He not only threw away the toy, he first broke it and laughed at it. The moment he walked away, he forgot all about it and never tried to find it or fix it. Why care for something that is not needed anymore? Its role in his life was over, or so I felt

I am more than sure that she is still out there. I do not remember the street I spotted her; I won't be able to locate her even if I fly to Amsterdam tomorrow. Nonetheless, I am not giving up. I plead for your help. This is a silver alert at the verge of despair. Help me find her! I believe that there were others who noticed her too. Please anyone... Even if you haven't seen her before; if you are in Amsterdam or planning a visit... Keep your eyes open, she is out there and I would like to know your side to this story.

Christina Demertsidou *is a Royal Holloway, University of London's MA Marketing with distinction graduate and a BA (Hons) Business Administration graduate of University of Portsmouth. Lived five years in the UK and during that time won various commendations/publications for poems and prose by participating at Tonguefreed, a Creative Writing in a Foreign Language competition. Since 2014 has been thrice short-listed at EYELANDS's International Short Story Contest and one of her stories has been published at Eyelands.gr as well. While in 2017 she also participated at EYELANDS's photo contest. Her photo entry was used as a cover for that contest's publication. In 2016 a short story written in Greek was published in an anthology by Bythebook. In 2017 she received the first prize and in 2018 the second prize at the international writing contest of EPOK. Both entries were in Greek language.*

Hunter
Mariam Syrengelas

-Good morning sir!

The curtains are pulled apart, the breakfast tray deposited at the foot of the bed.

-Your barber and manicurist are waiting.

The bedcovers groan and the man who emerges is still young, head tousled, scratching at his beard, naked, black eyes hooded from sleep, shaded by dark lashes.

-Again?

-It seems your hair and nails grow with remarkable rapidity.

His master sniffs daintily at his breakfast tray, holding up a red glass.

-Tomato-juice. You have a nine o'clock appointment at the bank, an eleven with your attorney and a lunch date.

-It's the hunting Thomas. It's a wonder I have any nails at all. He licks at the rim of the glass and downs the red liquid. That will be all Thomas.

-I shall take care of the birds sir. Save the best for dinner, hand the rest to the servants. Have a good day sir, and the butler steps smartly out of the room.

John Farmian stares at the mirror and his face stares back at him with blood-shot eyes, purple-lined from sleeplessness, his beard grizzly while unkept hair grows under his chin, trickling down his neck. He runs a hand through his hair, a bush thick and curling that grows to his shoulders and no comb can penetrate. His hands are torn by brush and brambles and thorns, the nails filthy, broken, ravaged. He rings for the barber and manicurist. It is now six. By eight thirty he will be a new man.

The rest of his day goes as planned. He sips the champagne and falls upon the beef cooked so that the blood seeps out mingling in the thin sauce and smiles discussing the day's stock-market. And when he is finished and strides out of the restaurant many a murmur follow. He is the eleventh richest man it is said, unmarried, unhindered by family, surrounded by loyal servants, business associates, by women; it is said he chooses his women carefully, discarding them tenderly and this last thing, along with his money, makes him well liked.

Outside, he walks swiftly stopping once to gaze at the window of a butcher shop. He has it all. Looks, dashing and daring, even forbidding at times but that could be on account of his huge fortune and the responsibilities that come with: tenants, board-meetings, of living in a house of forty-three rooms, which stands on the edge of the forest, overlooking the bare blue hills where no one ever goes. He lives alone with Thomas and a handful of servants, but his parties are lavish and splendid and he shows his guests the grounds, finally leading them to his stables, walking them along the handsome stalls, laughing as the dog-hounds wail in their darkened kernels like devils at a solstice dance.

He is a careful lover; considering and caring and tender, with the inbred knowledge that every body is beautiful, that each new body, deserves his sweet caresses, the patient, probing ministrations that will lead it finally to its peak of pleasure. He carefully twists his lovers' hair back and away so that he may watch their faces spasm with the agony of ecstasy. That may be the moment he loves them the most. He is careful of his women, as careful as he is of his choice of prey when happily hunting for, with the eye of the expert, he picks those which best suit his appetites. And so, when about to kill he chooses his new lover, not a virgin, but from those who have already experienced a cycle of at least a eight or nine years; whose bodies quiver in anticipation as young, once-a-month-cleansed blood courses through them electrifying them, flushing their cheeks and breast-tips. By and by, experience taught him to look for the dark long hair that reflects the light, for ivory teeth, for the dark-pink gums of health, for the glint and faintly wet sheen of the eye-ball; he looks for a stance that is upright, for a springy step, for a proud turn of the head. Under the guise of a kiss his nose twitches inhaling his lover's odor, his heart beats faster as the blood rushes in their veins only inches away from his lips.

He does not kill often though. Once every five is enough to keep him alive and the rest of the time he is more than content with his diet of almost raw vegetables and meat and crusty bread to mop up the remnants of blood in his plate. He kills on nights between moons, when the darkness is complete and the wolves silent and the stars too small to cast shadows. He then carries the bloodless victim to the hills, running easily, to his cousins, and sits with them smoking a cigarette while they devour the girl: the bones are broken and licked clean, crunched into dust by fangs like millstones, the clothes and hair torn to shreds and thrown in the meagre fire. He sits to smoke a second cigarette, a cub asleep in his lap, before leaving, and they know he'll be back again soon.

It is time to go hunting now. He hunts bare-handed, naked, sniffing out his small prey, grabbing for them in the dark as his yellow eyes blind and freeze them to the spot, in a split-second of terror before his fangs tear into them. He hunts small animals, edible, pheasants and fowl mostly, a fox at times and once, he could not resist, a boar. He dragged it home with him and the servants ate for a week for it was humongous, the weight of five men after it was skinned.

-My horse Thomas.

-The stable-man is ill. His niece shall bring her out.

He goes to the stable-yard but the girl takes a long time bringing out the gray mare and his temper is short.

-You're late, he snaps and mounts easily.

The mare circles impatient and gently she takes hold of the mouthpiece to steady her. She pats the strong neck and the horse nuzzles against her, nostrils flaring and the girl sniffs, lingering into the mare's mane, black hair mingling with gray mane-strands.

Farmian pulls at the horse's mouth, tugs it up and away from the girl's embrace and she looks up green eyes flashing, her lip curling over white teeth.

-Come ride with me.

They ride out side by side. She is tall and lanky, finely boned with narrow hips like a boy and she rides well, her strong body following the horse's movement fluidly as she rocks lightly on her saddle.

-Tomorrow!

-Yes sir.

-Do you have a name?

-Angelika.

Sweet, strange angel astride a horse.

So they ride every day. They traverse the dark woods and ride up the bare hills following, he knows, the wolf-trails but she seems unaffected by the silence. One evening, on the wood's edge they meet a she-wolf and feed her but as the beast growls over the meat, her horse, terrified, rears and throws her. She lands on thorns and sharp stone and cradles her hand in pain. He kneels to examine the wound; her palm is gnashed and he bends his head to suck the oozing blood, licking red drops until the flow stops. Her cheek is grazed and so he kisses away the red pearls of blood until she turns her head so that he is kissing her lips and then her mouth hurriedly and suddenly hungry until her teeth nip him and close sharply over his tongue with a hunger of her own; he feels the pain and pulls smartly away. This is new to him, this rush of sensation...... This.....Angelica.

So it begins. They come together, their bodies lunging at one another with the intensity of fanatics, their touch eager, hurried, seeking, like that of the truly blind. They make love in the forest, in deep foliage where she receives him, opening up, their lust wild, unabated, unsated by repetition as she writhes, closing about him, her nails digging his back, her teeth seeking his shoulder. But he always pulls way and she moans as he holds her off and down.

His passion for her is real and so he goes through his day half tumescent for each minute leads him closer to her. At nights he awakens to find himself painfully ready, swollen so that he roams the stables-yards, climbs her window and is at last inside of her. She always receives him, pulsing to his beat and he thrusts deep within her with the force of a beast, tearing at her, reaching that unfathomable place no one has ever found and she arches high, flamelike in her pleasure, so that he holds her immobile, his eyes a dark and sinister. Unsated, he dominates, pulling her hands back, tying them and she is at his mercy as, unbeknownst, he is at hers, as pain folds and molds into unbearable pleasure.

53

And then, the peace that comes with that fiery release of hormones rushing through their bodies, driving them into that illuminated darkness which clouds the senses, yet awakens, sparking every nerve-ending, every synapse, every touch. And when they are done, she cradles her lover, caressing his cheeks, the dark beard that circles face, fingers tracing the fine hairs soft and thick as fur. A face hard and shadowy angular, the face of something wild softened in repose, finally asleep. She knows his embrace can crush her easily but his fingers move over her like dark petals, cool like tears.

The moon is half and dwindling; a white sliver that hardly gives any light at all and he watches terrified. It is time and although he has no qualms about killing his heart-strings tug inexplicably at the thought of her dead. A world without her body walking through it holds no interest, no reason and his loins already ache at the thought of so imminent a loss. He weeps over her sleeping body, racked by sobs of yearning which lack the release of tears.

The night comes dark, with no moon, the stars-light edges of glass, too small to cast shadows. And he goes to her unable to resist destiny's tug and pull, baring his fangs where saliva glistens and clings in threads, but she laughs, her voice trilling and pushes him away and down, guiding his head and then holding it there upon her fragrant triangle of a forest. For a moment he is bewildered and then his nose twitches ecstatically and he buries his head in her heady, heavy shadows and laps it up greedily sending her into a frenzy "I love you, love youloveyouloveyou...". He keeps her clean for four days and nights, hiding under her skirts during the day, crawling after her in the stables, at nights opening her legs lovingly, delirious, hungry for her as she lays back, the white neck stretched out as if in offering, her nails racking his back and shoulders.

The first sliver of the new moon and the blood stops but he is free finally for he knows that each new month will bring new blood for him to feast upon and quench his thirst. He can have his pie and eat it too, not even his wildest dreams had held such a possibility. They fall upon each other ravenous, insatiable, lovers whose love, they know, shall now be forever. For the first time he knows the sweet twist of pain into pleasure as she drags her nails down his back leaving thin bloody trails; and he watches her eyes flash and close into yellow slits as she spasms in that final breath and frenzy of sweet and salient ecstasy and he enters her again, his body hard and lean as a wolf's.

-Sir, you shall be late again.

But he is exhausted, eyes ringed and furrowed in darkening purple shadows and he falls back too tired to speak.

-When did you last go a-hunting sir?

But he has fallen asleep, snorting gruffly.

He summons his attorney to draw up the necessary documents. He keeps the ruby ring in his pocket, the red cape wrapped.

54

The moon is full. They stroll through the gardens around midnight, their shadows at their heels, the house, rising like a rock behind them. Clouds part following a dying wind. He steps before her, stumbles, but only for a moment before he gracefully falls to his knees, one palm pressed upon his heart, breathless. She has never seen him loose his balance before.

-Will you marry me?

-John?

-Marry me!

He slips the ruby on her finger kissing the beloved open palm. He gives her the parcel exultant in his triumph but lies back gasping to rest against a tree trunk. He watches her undress, unfold the cloak, clasp it to her neck. And the wind comes again shaking the trees and the cloak bellows out, surrounds her, black-red and glistening in the moon-light like fresh blood. She is naked and pale, as he growls in craving and springs forward, greedy and unheeding of all but her, attacking her, throwing her to the ground. But she is his, opening up to receive him, closing about him fervent and fierce, like a vice of flesh and, when their moment comes, her teeth sink deep into his shoulder drawing his blood and he has no strength to pull away.

Lying together she caresses her lover's face, tracing the furry beard but under her fingers it comes away in tufts revealing a boy's smooth face, soft and unlined. In the cold light he trembles and shivers, suddenly too weak, his ribs sticking out as he hugs himself. She stares at him, this stranger, this feverish boy who stares back at her with love-sick eyes, a supplicant and she shies away in disgust throwing the cloak over him. Gratefully he wraps it about him thinking she is trying to keep him warm and reaches for her hand to kiss but she snatches it away, licking the last traces of his blood from her mouth. He looks at her uncomprehending: "Kiss me.", but she is backing away. "Come here!" he orders but his voice is whiny, pleading, her eyes yellow with unspoken anger. He stumbles to his feet, a thin, stringy youth, his member shriveled shamefully, knees knocking, reaching for her with trembling fingers and she pushes and kicks him in the ribs until he falls to the ground hugging himself, whimpering pitifully. She stares at him in disdain, hatefully, this stranger, steps over him and trots into the night forest to join the howling wolf-pack.

He is sick and weak, his blood poisoned by hers. The malady, he knows now, is irreversible. In the underbrush he scuttles in filthy rags, his frail body wounded and scabbed as he goes after the rats and small rodents that keep him alive. He sucks their blood, spitting out in disgust the hairs and bits of flesh that lodge between his teeth, throwing them away as soon as the last drop of blood is gone. A field mouse runs by and he lunges after it ungainly, but he is too slow, too tired and sprawls in the mud on all fours to watch it disappear through tall grass tail a-twitch.

55

Bouzouki Magic
Diane R. Ransdell

Our last day had been a marathon of stylobates and stelae, but the professor had promised that our last night would be a highlight. The university tour always culminated with a feast on the Plaka, the hill that cradled the Acropolis, which we'd visited the day before.

From our hotel on Mitropoleos, Jon walked us around the corner to Mnisikleous. To-gether the twenty-six of us started marching up the hill.

When my girlfriend Selma and I had tried the same route the night before, the restaurant sharks had been so vicious that we'd given up and eaten at Not Just Falafel. With Jon as our leader, the sharks knew to back away.

"Best place in Athens," Jon told us as we kept climbing. "You'll see."

The three-week trip had been the best choice of my undergraduate career. I'd picked up six credits and made a good friend. We'd be flying home in the morning. By the fol-lowing month I probably wouldn't remember the difference between Doric and Corinthian columns. I might confuse the photos I took at Delphi with the ones I took at Olympia. But I would come away with a taste of five thousand years of Greek history. For a first trip to Europe, that was the most I could have hoped for.

"Rachel, what did you like the best?" Jon asked as I panted beside him. I wanted to tell him was the truth: What I liked the best was the way he would hop off the bus at a place like Mycenae and shout, "It doesn't get any better than this!" He would dance around with his arms held high in the air as if thanking the Greek gods for their ingenuity. The sites were amazing: the theater at Epidaurus, the fortress at Nauplion, the palace at Knossós. But what resonated the most was my professor's own enjoyment. I couldn't quite appreciate the simplicity of a Cycladic statue or the historical significance of a Bronze Age gate, yet I felt how much Jon wanted me to. I loved him for those joyous touches, his absolute fascination with everything he was showing us. For three weeks he'd been a dedicated tour guide, and he deserved our thanks and appreciation, and may-be a stiff Greek drink.

"Rachel?"

"There's too much to choose from!"

"I know. But one thing."

"Sounion, then. If I really had to say."

Jon smiled as he kept walking. It was lame to choose the highlight from the day be-fore, but my professor understood why. We'd caught the site at dusk, and golden light had danced on the stones.

"Where will you go for your next trip?" he asked.

My mom's parents were Mexican and my dad's were Italian. So maybe my next destination should be Cancún or Milan?Neither answer seemed appropriate for the ears of an archaeology professor.

"First I'll have to pay off my credit card."

"Yes, yes. And after that?"

"I'll start looking for airfare."

"Good idea," he said. "Good idea indeed. But first, let's eat!"

Jon pointed to a taverna on the left side of the street named O Geros tou Moria, (The Old Man of Peloponesus). He herded us towards the center of a rectangular room where ourplac-es had already been set. Three waitersand the owner rushed to help, greeting us warmly. I dragged Selma to the head of the table before anyone could stop us. I wasn't trying to beat out my companions, but I wanted to get as close to the front as possible. I didn't care about the kitchen on the right or the open-air walls on the left. I wanted to be near the stage.

Four chairs were set up in a line. Two held guitars. The other two held bouzoukis. Three men huddled behind the chairs, leisurely preparing for the evening. They were older than the professor. One had white hair. The other two were younger, maybe fifty-something. All werewell-tanned by the summer sun, a clear benefit of having a night job.

"The taramosalata is excellent here," Jon said. "The moussaka is the best in the city. For those of you with no imagination, the gyros and souvlakia are excellent choices as well."

The fourth man arrived, and the musicians sat. The leader turned out to be the bouzouki player who sat on the second chair. He nodded briefly, and the quartet began an upbeat tune.

"Your order, miss?" asked the waiter.

"What's the name of this song?"

The young man turned around, unimpressed. "Varka sto gialó."

"Which means?"

"'The Boat on the Beach.' Your order?"

For a country such as Greece, the song title was perfect. The happy melody skipped along with all the men singing in unison.

"Should I come back?" the waiter asked.

I couldn't be bothered with the menu. I chose the souvlakia. Then I swiveled my chair to face the stage. I tuned out everything around me to concentrate on the bright harmonies of my first live bouzouki band.

Jon leaned over. "Can you catch any of the words?"

For the past three weeks I'd been glued to my phrasebook. Since I spoke Spanish, I'd assumed I could easily pick up some Modern Greek. Instead the language was much harder than I'd anticipated.The word for "please" consisted of four syllables; the word for "thanks" required three.

57

"I can't understand a thing!"

"That's all right. For Greek songs, it's easy. M'agapás, s'agapó. You love me, I love you. That's all you need to know. Say, don't you play in a mariachi band?"

I nodded.

"Violin?"

A mariachi was a band that included a violin, a trumpet, a vihuela, and a guitarrón. I nodded again. "That's right."

"So this group is like the one you have back home?"

A mariachi was a noisy exclamation of joy. The rhythm instruments played against each other while the trumpets and violins had fencing duels. We played huapangos and sones, usually in major keys.

"It sounds almost exactly the same."

He laughed as he turned towards the other students and left me alone to settle into the music. The songs were cheerful and snappy or slow and tormented, laments as well as celebrations. Often I heard s'agapó or m'agapás. But I didn't need to understand the words to understand the attitude. The four musicians were doing their best to transport the diners to wherever they needed to go.

It wasn't until the fifth or sixth song that the band members took note of me. They weren't startled by someone who was genuinely paying attention to their work. Instead they nodded and smiled. Obviously, I wasn't flirting with all four of them at once; actually, I wasn't flirting with any of them at all. My affair was with the music, and they understood that too. Because no matter that the songs had unfamiliar tempos or that the harmonies were dissonant and complex, the musicians and I were one and the same. We might have lived continents apart, but if they'd held up a mirror, I would have been on the other side.

Selma tapped me on the shoulder and indicated the stage. "So are they cute or are they good?"

"They probably used to be cute. But they're very experienced."

"They play well?"

Selma wasn't a musician. She'd never studied music. I didn't have a way to explain that since I'd never heard live bouzouki music, I couldn't judge the group's quality, not accurately. I'd only heard two or three of the songs before such as "Never on Sunday." I'd seen pictures of bouzouki bands that included drumsets or keyboards, which would have given a different and fuller flavor to the men's work. All that seemed too complicated to break down.

"They've played with one another so long that they can anticipate the next songs," I said. I pointed to the leader. "That one usually calls the shots, but if he's distracted by customers, the other bouzouki player takes over and starts without him. I wouldn't say that one is better than the other. They seem to trade solo licks. Either way they seem perfectly comfortable, which tells me they've played these songs hundreds of times."

"What about the guitar players?"

"Watch the way they strum at exactly the same time."

"Isn't that usual?"

I thought of my own group, where the guitarrón player tended to drag and the vihuela player tended to rush. "In theory, yes. In practice, no."

They'd all started a rebétiko at exactly the same moment.

"I don't like that guy's voice," Selma said. "It sounds like he's complaining."

"Well, he is!"

"You can understand what he's singing?"

"I can guess the gist. Rebétika are complaints about society. They became popular in the 60s or so when a lot of people were out of work."

"They're supposed to sound ugly?"

"No. But they give people the chance to release their emotions."

"Like when those guys danced all funny?"

The whole taverna had noticed the two men who rose to perform the drunken angel dance. "Yes. Same idea. Dance out your emotions. Get everything out of your system instead of locking it inside."

"Instead of yelling at one another like in my family?"

"Or like in mine! This is a little different. It's more internal, retrospective."

"Watch out! It sounds like you're turning into a Greek philosopher."

"Don't worry. There's no chance of that."

The comment was flippant. Songs themselves were philosophical. Usually they suggested deep concepts in simple phrases. I could have provided Selma with countless examples. When I sang Juan Gabriel's "No vale la pena," "It's Not Worth the Trouble," I thought back on every bad boyfriend I'd wasted time on. When I sang "Costumbres," "Customs," I chided myself for lingering in a broken relationship instead of taking action. I could have spent all night explaining to Selma how Mexican songs were all philosophical statements and argued that the Greek songs were undoubtedly the same, even if a lot of them talked about love. But such a discussion would have eaten valuable listening time.

"So you're not bored?" Selma asked.

I checked my watch. "It's nearly midnight, yet the only song they've repeated so far was a request for 'The Zorba Dance.' That means they have a huge repertoire. It also means they've been playing three hours straight without a break. That's amazing."

The players back home would have revolted. We were paid to play hour-long sets, but my companions were thrilled if they got away with playing fifty minutes instead.

"You're basically sitting here all alone."

It was true that half the students had left, and the others had bunched up around Jon as they ordered more Metaxá, Greek brandy.

"Efxaristó. Thanks for noticing. But I've never been less alone." I wanted to add, "or felt more alive," but again, it was too hard to explain. The band had started a particularly haunting song, and I didn't want to miss a single chord.

"Are you coming?" Jon asked.

When I turned around, I realized that my companions were standing and stretching their legs. By now it was well past midnight, and they were prepared to call it a night.

"Do I have to?"

"Not at all." We surveyed the room. The tourists were long gone, but several noisy Greek families had wandered in, and they were loudly voicing favorite requests.

"There are several empty tables, so there's no problem. You remember the way back to the hotel?"

"Down the street to the bottom and turn right."

"Exactly. You don't mind staying by yourself?"

"I prefer it. And thanks for the terrific evening."

Jon smiled. "I knew you would enjoy it more than the others."

As I turned around, I winked at the lead bouzouki player, and he winked back. He appreciated my interest as much as I appreciated that he loved his job. He had mastered the evening and offered us the best of his magical world.

Thus here in Athens' Plaka, I had come home. I had found my kindred spirits. No matter the dance rhythms or the chord progressions, these men were my brothers. We were devoted to the same gods. It didn't matter that we couldn't speak to one another or that I wasn't able to play along. I understood my fellow musicians as well as if we'd been swapping stories all evening. When they were asked to play "The Zorba Dance" yet again, I imagined playing "Cielito lindo" for the zillionth time. When they paused to stretch their hands, I could feel the weariness of their fingers, the tension in their wrists. When they reached for more water, I noticed that my glass was dry.

But Jon had erred. The farewell feast hadn't been amere highlight. It had been the zenith of my entire vacation. By experiencing a bouzouki band, the world had become a continuous circle. Even though I was a tiny wheel, I recognized my foothold in the vastness of the universe.

Where would I go for my next vacation? The question was ludicrous because I would start making plans to return even before I left. As long as I could hear live folk music, I would feel right at home. But first I would prepare by taking language classes. I would find recordings and study lyrics. I might even learn basics about the bouzouki. Then I would make my plans. Whether I traveled to the north or to the south, within the main-land or among the islands, I would hurry back to Apollo's playground. To Hellas. To Greece.

*It only took one night at a taverna for **D.R. Ransdell** to fall in love with bouzouki music, especially since it reminded her of the Mexican tunes she played back in Arizona. The Greek lyrics were so mysterious and intoxicating that she soon enrolled in Modern Greek. For the next decade she traveled to the country each summer, exploring different beaches, reveling in folk music, and battling her way through Greek. When she landed a job at a language school in Rhodes Town, she signed on for year.While completing graduate studies, she found that writing about Greece was a vital mental vacation; she could travel to the country for free night after night. In her first novel, Amirosian Nights, Rachel Campanello finds that haunting melodies, moonlit beaches, and a handsome bouzouki player spice up a summer holiday. In Island Casualty, mariachi violinist Andy Veracruz turns amateur detective to learn how a lost engagement ring leads to dangerous midnight Vespa rides.For more information, please see www.dr-ransdell.com.*

5 2 12
Charles Osborne

Arianna nervously looked at her watch. It was nearly 12.00. She wondered whether her lunch date would turn up.

A few days earlier a fire had broken out at the Tivoli, a nightclub in the centre of town. By the time the fire and rescue services arrived, the fire had taken hold and engulfed the roof. Flames shot up high into the midnight air. The firemen reeled out their hoses, manned their extended ladders, and fought hard to control the blaze. Others smashed their way into the blazing building. The firemen fought all night to get the blaze under control. By morning, a group of blackened firefighters sat exhausted and dejected on a couple of dilapidated wooden benches fronting the old town hall.

Arianna lived nearby. Her father was dead a year now. He had held an important job in Athens before his early retirement. He had been a serious-minded man dedicated to hard work. Her mother, on the other hand, was from a well-off family from urban Italy. They made an odd couple. Arianna took after her mother in that she was full of vigour and Italian charm. Arianna cheekily managed to make her way through the police cordon. As she reached the café where she worked, she could see the devastation in front of her. The Tivoli was a smoking shell, almost burnt to the ground. Arianna rolled up her sleeves and set to work. Soon she was ferrying steaming hot cups of tea and coffee to the exhausted firefighters. There was a small space on one of the benches. She edged herself in between two young firefighters. They looked no older than her twin brother. So young to be in such a responsible job she thought. She asked one of the firefighters sitting next to her about the fire. He slowly took off his helmet to reveal his blackened face, He told her that, sadly, there had been several fatalities, all young people. A tear welled in his eyes and trickled down his blackened face. She reached for his hand. He was trembling.

At exactly midday, her date came rushing up, panting for breath.
   'Just made it,' he gasped.
   'I thought you weren't coming,'
   'Oh, I always keep a promise, especially for...'
   'Come on, let's see if there's a spare table,' Arianna quickly interjected, not wanting her date to embarrass himself.
   'Hello, Justin. Who's your lady friend?' asked the manager.
   'This is Arianna, who was our little angel on the day of the nightclub fire.'

'Pleased to meet you. I've heard so much about you.'

Arianna blushed.

The manager ushered them to an alcove table set for two, with newly laundered napkins and a little vase of fresh-cut flowers.

'I thought your name was John.'

'Well Arianna, you've found me out.'

'It's all very mysterious,' teased Arianna. 'You haven't got something to hide have you?

'Oh, no. there's a fairly simple explanation really.'

'Which is?'

'You know you wondered whether I was coming or not.'

'Well, you did just make it', joked Arianna.

'And that's the answer. I'm always arriving just in time.'

'So?'

'Well, the fire crew were always ribbing me about arriving just in time, so they christened me Justin for short, and the name stuck.'

'Well it suits you. I rather like it.'

'It once saved my life, you know.'

'How was that, John, or should I say Justin?'

'You can call me Justin if you want to. All my friends do.'

'Justin sounds nice. So, Justin it is.'

Arianna took a sip of her hot sweetened coffee. 'You were going to explain.'

'Not sure I really want to,' replied Justin. 'It's a bit of a bad memory.'

'That's all right,' whispered Arianna. 'I quite understand.' 'Was it to do with your job?'

'Yes, it was,' replied Justin, after a brief pause.

Arianna didn't know whether to drop the topic, but she was intrigued. 'Was it to do with that huge forest fire last year,' she gently persisted.

'How did you know?'

'Just a guess.'

'By the time I got to the fire station just in time for my afternoon shift,' Justin continued, 'the first fire tender had already left the station.'

'But that's not your fault if you were on time, even if only just.'

'Yes, I know. But the thing is that the men on that fire tender never came back.'

Arianna could feel his pain. 'That must have been devastating.'

I found It difficult to live with myself after that. I had to seek counselling,' confided Justin.

'Oh, Justin. How terrible.'

'I wouldn't want anything like that to happen to you, Arianna.'

63

'I'm sure it won't.'

Justin felt the need to change the topic. 'Would you like an aperitif?'

'Oh, yes. That would be nice.'

'Look, I have an idea,' suggested Justin, intriguingly.

'And what is that?'

'Well, keep this to yourself,' confided Justin, 'but, in an extreme emergency, we and the other emergency services, such as the police and ambulance service, together with top local officials, have to rendezvous at a secret bunker buried deep underground.'

'Excuse my naivety, Justin, but what has this got to do with me?'

'Well, it's like this. The authorities are looking for someone reliable and discreet to provide catering services in the event of an emergency, and I thought you might fit the part.'

'But I'm only a part-time waitress,' explained Arianna.

'Don't worry. I'll see if I can pull a few strings,' insisted Justin.

A week or so later, Arianna received a summons to attend the town hall. The mayor was there to greet her. What had started out as an interview turned into something more like an interrogation. Her whole life history was examined in detail. Her educational achievements, her financial circumstances, her employment history, whom she associated with, her political and religious views, her interests and pastimes were all gone over with a fine-tooth comb. Her rather left-leaning political and environmental views seemed to count against her. However, when she mentioned that her late father had been a former member of the diplomatic service their attitude changed.

The next day Arianna met Justin at the town square. He had two bikes with him.

'Here, hop on,' he gestured.

'Where are we going?'

'You'll see.'

They got on the bikes and headed out through the outskirts of town into the surrounding countryside. Justin was going at a fast pace and Arianna was having difficulty keeping up with him.

'How much further?' she asked after several kilometres.

'Hang on, we're nearly there.'

They dismounted and wheeled their bikes down a steep remote path to the bottom of a huge disused quarry. Along one of the walls of the quarry was a disguised door.

'Here, I've got something for you.'

'What's that?'

'It's your new special security pass. Here give it a try.'

'Don't I need a password?'

'No, it's a facial and fingerprint recognition system.' explained Justin. 'Here, I'll show you.'

A door opens. Once inside, they descend in a huge lift deep into the bowels of the earth. Below are a range of police vehicles, ambulances, fire engines, bulldozers and other machinery lined up in neat rows. While off to one side is a large control room with banks of computers, printers, and telephones. On the other are offices, an eating area, and sleeping quarters. Justin and Arianna stroll over to the eating area.

'Here, this is where you'll be working if they need you. What do you think?'

'It seems very well equipped,' exclaims Arianna, 'but a bit scary.'

Arianna returned to waitressing. Life moved slowly along. The Tivoli was rebuilt. But then things changed overnight. The last flight had left. The airport was closed. All trains had stopped. There were few buses and even fewer cars. Garages were closed and fuel was running out. Angry crowds were besieging the town hall and other public buildings. The scenes were growing ugly. Several buildings were set on fire. Justin was called in to help extinguish the fires and to assist the police in holding back the angry crowds. It was not until around 11.00 p.m. in the evening that the crowds drifted away. People flocked to the churches. Prayers were offered up. It was time for Justin to take his leave.

Working transport was scarce, if almost non-existent. Luckily, Justin had an old modified Vespa scooter from the 1960's which he was restoring. Restoration was far from complete, but it would have to do. The scooter was just about roadworthy. It had little fuel. Would it get them there?

Justin met Arianna at 11.30 p.m. She was reluctant to leave. The night was pitch dark and eerily silent.

'Come on,' he insisted.

Arianna hesitated.

'Come on, hop on. We haven't got much time.'

The Vespa spluttered into life, and they were off.

Justin drove as fast as he could, zigzagging between abandoned and broken-down cars and lorries. The engine coughed and spluttered. And finally gave up.

'Are we nearly there,' asked Arianna.

'About another half a kilometre. We'll have to run for it.'

'When is the asteroid due to hit?'

'Around midnight.'

'What's the time now?

'5 to 12.'

The back wedding dress
Ilona krueger

Helga Seidel threw her book on the floor. Two hours of trying to come to terms with page one was quite enough. She looked at her watch. Half-an-hour before midnight. Her mind, a cacophony of everything happening in her life currently, could not be stilled. Sadness about recent events shadowed her but excitement at upcoming created the see-saw. In a week she would be a married woman. In a few hours, she would be telling Matthias the secret she was carrying within her.

Sleep was as elusive as a butterfly darting into flowers to sip delightful nectars. Earlier in the evening, she, herself, had enjoyed a small glass of mead with dinner, whilst listening to the solo-violinist play *Eine Kleine Nachtmusik*, her favourite piece. When offered a second glass, she had regretfully declined but knew it was for the best. There would be time for that later.

Helga kept checking the time. A watched pot never boils, her mother would always say. She'd only been away for a month but it was a month too long. Matthias would be waiting for her at the station and their embrace would be long and warm.

She remembered her first day at school in Bremen. Herr Wolfe had instructed her to sit next to Matthias. At ten years of age, sitting next to a boy was probably the most irksome thing she could imagine. It was the only seat available, so she perched herself at the far end of the seat, avoiding any accidental contact. Matthias had watched her wipe her pencil thoroughly after he had picked it up off the floor for her, clearly amused.

'I have very clean germs, you know. They are very well behaved,' he whispered.

Unable to stifle her own laugh quickly enough, Helga clapped her hands over her mouth.

'This is a classroom, not a playground, Fräulein Seidel. Please keep that in mind. Keller, pay attention to your work,' Herr Wolfe snapped. Exchanged glances and smiles sealed their friendship. Helga moved more comfortably to the middle of the seat. They sat together at recess.

'Budapest is a long way from Bremen. Why were you there?'

'Because of my father's work. He is Hungarian.'

'And your mother?'

'My parents divorced. She has family here, in Germany.'

'Do you miss your father?'

'Every day. But he has promised to send for me during holidays.'

But the promises fell by the wayside.

His new wife didn't want the inconvenience of another man's brat. In fact, she didn't even want brats of her own. Life had more to offer than snotty-nosed kids. The Opera, travel, parties and anything wild, glamorous and expensive. Helga read the new Frau Seidel's letter over and over without her mother ever knowing she had found the hiding spot. Her heart was wrung out like an old tea-towel but she pretended otherwise. She waited. Hoped and waited.

Her hopes crumbled over time. No news, despite letters to him clearly labelled with her address, her phone number within.

Nothing for twenty years.

The hospital had called. He'd suffered a stroke, but was stable. He wanted to see his daughter.

The dagger in her chest twisted. She was bleeding inside. A physical wound could not compare. Helga had become accustomed to his absentia, having long since quelled her pain, pacified the resentment and thwarted her anger. The game of volleyball in her life, where the ball was a huge grenade, was too dangerous.

'Deal with it,' Mattie had said, when she mentioned the call from the hospital. ' 'Forgive him, Helga. He's your father, for goodness sake. You just never what burdens people shoulder.'

'And mine?'

'Be the brave one, take the plunge. Don't set yourself up for regret.'

The lopsided, but delighted, smile on her father's face melted away the years. His words were slurred and awkward when they came, but his voice cracked and his eyes glistened as he said, "I have missed every day of your absence.' He said so much more, more than her heart could hold. The penultimate moment had arrived. A cupful of water can only hold so much before it overflows. Her tears flowed till the reservoir was dry. Three weeks later, they flowed again when her father lapsed into his final coma, leaving Helga and the mortal world behind.

The train continued its white noise chugging, clattering and rattling, seemingly, with a life and dialogue of its own. Hypnotised, Helga's head began to nod like a tired poppy. That delightful time of reverie before succumbing to sleep was upon her… finally. She was floating in a distant field of dreams when a sudden jolt snapped her back into reality. How long had she slept?

Five minutes to Midnight. She closed her eyes again, anticipating a return to the kaleidoscope of mellow meadows, sunshine and smiles. However, an icy chill gathered around her, causing her to shudder. Helga perceived she was not alone. Dare she open her eyes?

The she heard it.

'Widow's Bridge,' it said softly but drawn-out like a record played on slow speed. 'The moon will receive its sacrifice.'

What in God's name! She slapped herself awake and scanned the compartment. No-one in there. Her dream had morphed into a nightmare. Helga dared not go back to sleep. If only it were daytime, so that she could watch the passing landscape. Peering out, head against the glass pane, visibility was surprisingly good. As the train snaked around a bend, the moon came into view. A huge golden moon. A full moon.

She heard it again.

'Widow's Bridge.' This time it was more of a snarl. She envisaged a dog, perhaps a wolf, baring its teeth in warning and menace.

Had the mead gone to her head? Was there truth in the notion of full moon lunacy? She had read about it often enough in case studies of psychiatric patients. A fascinating subject, but was she now a victim? Or was it, perhaps it was the hormones tossing around her emotions. Mattie had noticed her ambivalence a few times, even though she hadn't yet mentioned her suspicions. An examination at the hospital in Budapest had verified her pregnant state. Only her father knew.

'I am going to be a grandfather. An Opa!' The moment was priceless. Helga hoped Heaven had windows with magnifying vision.

She envisaged the scene when she'd be telling Mattie her news. There would be stunned but delighted surprise. There would be laughter and joy, plans and arrangements. She could hardly wait to get home to her lifelong friend and love. And to their wedding.

'Widow's Bridge. Widow's Bridge.' That chilling voice. She saw the bridge. On the parapet, a figure. Sinister. Ghostly. She shivered again as an arctic breeze whipped at her.

Then came the scream. Bloodcurdling, from someone who wasn't there. And then weeping. Sad, sad weeping. Where was it coming from? Startled she took her focus away from the darkness outside, and she saw.

Across from her sat a woman, an old woman, tiny and fragile as though she would crumple at a whisper. Skin as translucent as a finely spun silk chemise. Delicate like a tiny violet, but weeping loudly as if she were outcrying the strings of a lamenting violin.

Helga gasped in alarm. Who was this woman? This transparent, frail woman wearing a long gown, out of the fashion annals. Elaborate like a wedding dress, rich with beading, lace and embroidered pintucks, complemented by a veil equally adorned: a work of art.

But it was black. A black wedding dress.

Helga didn't know what to do. Should she say something? Words evaded her. The ghost-like figure wasn't real, was it? It was only a figment of her pregnant mind, wasn't it? What if....? Helga felt the blood draining out her face and her breathing quickening. Her inner world sunk into momentary darkness, and as she came to, the macabre woman had gone.

There was no sign of her later, either, in the dining room, at breakfast. Still feeling light-headed and somewhat nauseous, Helga opted for a strong cup of tea and a serving of raisin toast. Upon asking the steward if he had seen a strange woman fitting the description of the old woman in the black dress, the reply was adamant, 'No, no, no. I have no knowledge of her.' And yet, apprehension stole across his face belying his words.

When he came back later to refill her cup, she quietly said, 'I saw her last night... in my compartment. Please tell me what you know.'

'I do not know anything. Perhaps you were dreaming.' His eyes shadowed. 'I'm sorry.'

Disappointed, Helga, finished her tea, but left her toast. Did he think she was crazy? A neurotic and overly imaginative woman? What would Mattie say when she told him her experience? Would he also think she was mad? Would he ask her if she'd had anything to drink? Ah, that explains it, he would say. Perhaps she should file this away with the other secrets. She did not want to spoil the celebration of their imminent marriage. Nor the celebration of the new life within her.

Many other guests were happily engrossed in conversation. Romantics holding hands. Suit-clad businessmen flicking through documents. Another professional-looking woman engaging in an agreement with an agent. Well-behaved children with coloured pencils and books. Another child pestering its mother with a barrage of questions.

'I told you, it won't be long now. Eat your breakfast and don't play with your food.'

'I don't like it and I am not going to eat it.'

'You'd better, otherwise no sweets when we get there.'

Bribery and blackmail starting early in a child's life! What kind of a parent did that? On second thought, Helga had to laugh, imagining she would probably be doing the same thing herself in the not-too-distant future. Judge and be judged, she thought as she got up to leave for her compartment. She needed to gather her things ready for the arrival back in Bremen. She smiled at people as she walked through the dining-cabin.

And then, but it couldn't be! Where….how…what? And why?

The familiar face of the Woman in the Black Wedding Dress stared at her in the same unnerving manner as the night before. Only for a moment, but yet a long enough, chilling enough to encrypt itself into Helga's mind forever. The woman then turned to the man beside her, adoring him with her eyes. A woman in love! Transformed, like the black dress now blanched into wedding-white. A princess in a happily-ever-after scenario. Vanished were the wrinkles of age. Gone was the malice of her earlier countenance. Instead, a beautiful woman with her whole life rolled out in front of her, like a rich carpet stretching forever.

What did all of this mean? Helga was seriously doubting her own sanity. Seeing things that no-one else saw. Hallucinations? Apparitions? Waking dreams?

Sleepwalking, perhaps? Whatever all this was, she'd be put into an asylum if she told anyone.

And then a scream that could drown out the sound of an avalanche of rocks, followed by mournful weeping. The handsome young man was no longer there. The woman was there alone, old, her dress once again black. A funeral bride.

Helga collapsed.

She woke in her cabin to a small group of people concerned for her well-being. 'I am okay, really I am. I should have finished my breakfast. Thank you, really, all is good.'

The steward was amongst the group. The others left when he promised to bring some more food. He did not leave immediately.

'I know what you saw.' He began. 'She shows herself at the same place each time on the anniversary of her bridegroom's suicide. He jumped off the bridge that has come to be known as Widow's Bridge, on the eve of their wedding. He was the love of her life but he was obviously troubled. Her wedding dress was never worn but she had a replica made in black. She wore that for the rest of her life. She was filled so much with grief and bitterness that she wished tragedy upon others. After her own death, the sightings began and each time they did, there was always a corresponding tragedy.'

A frozen chill slashed down Helga's spine. Fear exploded through her, but she kept calm in the exterior.

'How do you know all this?'

'She was my grandmother. My mother was born six months after this horrible ordeal.'

Helga listened, speechless. She wasn't crazy, but all of this was... too much to process.

'I shall get you some food. Will you manage by yourself? Or should someone sit with you?'

'No, no, I shall be fine,' she assured. She wore the mask till he was gone.

A powerful surge of angst struck. She saw her parallel life. Soon to be married, pregnant. The woman had come to her. Was it an omen? A foreboding of things to come? Trepidation pulsed in her chest. She argued with her mind. Matthias had everything going for him, a well-paying job that he liked, despite frequent late hours and sudden trips away. He had recently bought an enviable residence that they would share together. He had her devotion and love. They were happy. Very happy.

Realisation smacked her in the face, washing relief over her. The tragedy had already happened. Her long-lost father had died. It wasn't a premonition. It was a recognition of what had already happened. She had nothing to fear. Nothing at all.

Guards were helping people off the train. Where was Matty? He had arranged to meet her. Caught up with work no doubt. He wouldn't have forgotten.

'Would you be Helga Seidel?' the guard asked. When she replied that she was, he gave her the single rose and envelope with her name and train details on it. It was from Mattie! How wonderfully romantic he was. Her initial disappointment at not seeing him eased.

'My darling,' it read.

Helga smiled.

'We have always been best friends and that I love you is a certainty. There are so many things about you that I love.'

She glowed as she gathered in his words, blushing as she read about how remarkable she was.

'However, I cannot live with my secret any longer. I cannot give you the family you want, nor ever love you in that special private way husbands and wives do. For you see, I love men, and that is not acceptable in our society. Please forgive me. You deserve much better.'

The guard was still there. A Police Officer stepped forward. 'He left this on the bridge before jumping. No one could stop him. You have our deepest condolences, Miss Seidel.'

Helga heard the laughing. No-one else heard it, but she knew that voice.

The Midnight Show
Charles Venable

The air smelled like cheap liquor and cheaper cologne. A scrawny, white guy with wire-frame spectacles stumbled up to me with a glass of whiskey in one hand and Chantel's ass in the other. His nose and cheeks flushed red with booze.

"Do you play basketball?" He slurred.

I ignored him. Chantel flashed me an apologetic smile. She was pretty: too pretty for this dead beat. Her skin wasn't as dark as mine: not the color of coca-cola left to sit in the sun. Hers was closer to the whiskey in his glass, a warm amber. Tonight, she wore daisy dukes and a crop top; it was almost tasteful for this place.

"Hey, I'm talking to you," He shouted over the music.

She pulled on his arm, but he resisted. He wasn't a big man, but Chantel was five feet in her heels. Chantel's apologetic smile shifted to one of warning: if I threw out another of her customers, she'd never let me hear the end of it.

"Sorry," I said, "Couldn't hear you. What did you ask?"

"Do you play basketball?" The man repeated.

"Not anymore. Not since high school."

"Oh," He huffed, "Shame. How tall are you?"

"Six feet seven."

His eyes went wide, "Wow. You know, I used to play basketball, back in the day."

"That so?" I asked.

His question answered, he didn't resist Chantel's pull. Slowly, she drew him away, back into the crowd, towards the private rooms. Chantel flashed me a smile, and my heart skipped a beat.

Even after half as a bouncer for the Open Oyster Gentleman's Club & Bar, I wasn't used to being around beautiful women all the time, but the girls treated me wel. On the occasion when they smiled or thanked me, I felt like a teenager again.

There were thirteen girls, in total; a fact not lost on me, the owner, or the regulars. The Oyster had a reputation for bad luck: open for fifty years, it had closed and reopened eleven times and changed owners just as often: most had died. My favorite story was the chain-smoker who tried to turn the place into a gas station. He installed the tanks and pumps on the side of the building, but on the first delivery, blew himself to bits and took the brand new pumps and tanks with him. The guy after him turned the crater into a parking lot.

Plenty of parking, hot girls, and cheap booze attracted a lot of customers, and a lot of customers drinking cheap booze and watching hot girls got rowdy. The current owner hired me to replace the last bouncer, a short and stout ex-marine with so many tattoos his skin seemed darker than mine. He was still a regular, and he'd tell me stories on slow nights.

Tonight was not a slow night. Chantel was on her third private show. I glanced at the old clock set above the stage. It was eleven fifty-five. Almost time for Midnight's show. People filtered out of private rooms and through the front doors to find good spots by the front.

Closer to the stage, the smell of perfume replaced the cologne. It wasn't cheap stuff, either; the current owner gave the girls a bonus each month to buy their own. The only rule was no two girls had the same scent. It meant each girl had a distinct smell, a distinct flavor.

Midnight wore Boss No. 6, a man's cologne, and before her shows, one of the other girls spritzed the stage with it.

There were plenty of pretty girls at the Oyster, but Midnight was special. She was the star of the show. As the clocked ticked closer to 12:00, the crowd grew quiet, and the lights faded to crimson. The colors changed with her outfit and her song. Tonight, as the lights warmed, a high-energy hip-hop song throbbed from the speakers. Drinks rippled. One of the server girls passed too close to hand off a drink, and the dull bass ran through her breasts, earning a chorus of cheers from the men.

The lights flashed once, and the chorus became silent. The second flash turned the silence into a shiver in the air. All the men swayed and throbbed with excitement. The final flash accompanied the crescendo of the bass and the flutter of the curtains at the back of the stage as Midnight stepped proudly into view, illuminated in a halo of red light.

Without heels, she was as tall as me; I'd met her once, backstage, and she was the only person in the joint I ever looked at eye-to-eye. Tonight, she wore six inch stilettos: a glossy red gleaming in the light, drawing the eyes down legs wrapped in fish-net stockings, up to a matching leather skirt, Midnight was all legs. Chantel told me she was a swimmer in college, and I believed it. Her navel was pierced, and tonight, a single green stud stood out among the bright red. Her shirt was little more than a strip of black cloth around her breasts. Surprisingly, her breasts were small; she was almost flat chested, with only a hint of cleavage in her more teasing outfits. A red leather jacket draped over her shoulders, but her arms weren't in the sleeves.

As she came out, the tension in the air released in a hiss as everyone collectively exhaled, and in the second breath, a cheer rose up, her name called by the regulars who came exclusively to see her.

And it was no wonder why: the red lights turned her creamy skin a golden hue, glinting of sequins set in the shoulder of the jacket and glitter dusted generously on her cheeks. Her face was masculine: high cheekbones, a sharp nose and chin with a strong jawline, but she always highlighted her best features with clever use of makeup, drawing attention to hazel eyes and auburn hair.

On the stage, it seemed like she was on fire.

I milled around the back of the bar, keeping an eye on the patrons. Occasionally, there' d be an asshole who'd try to tug one off in the middle of a show. It was awkward throwing a guy with his cock hanging loose out of the bar, but it had to be done for the comfort of the girls and the other patrons. Once, there' d been a guy who fell asleep at his table. We'd moved him quietly to a private room until he woke up with a hangover six hours later.

Tonight, it was calm. A few rowdy fellows, like the weasel of a man Chantel was hosting in the back, but the rowdiness was directed towards Midnight as she swayed on the stage. When nobody stuck out among the crowd, I found a secluded spot by the wall and made myself comfortable.

One of the serving girls brushed past me, "Want anything?"

I shook my head, "I'm good for now."

Suddenly, a gasp rose from the crowd. Midnight was halfway off the stage; the hem of her skirt caught on the lip of the catwalk, revealing lacy black panties clinging tightly to the largest dick I'd ever seen in my life. A murmur ran through the crowd. A few patrons stood and walked out. Their footsteps were the first of the boos rumbling from the crowd. Midnight's face, already red from the burning lights, hid behind her hands.

I pushed through the aisles up to the stage. Already oa drunk leaned towards her. I pushed him back.

"Please stay behind the line."

The man fell back in his chair, eyes wide. Usually, my size was enough. I turned and found Midnight struggling to readjust her skirt with one hand while hiding her face with the other. I placed a hand cautiously on her shoulder and pointed to the curtain leading backstage. When she glanced up at me, her eyes were wet with tears. She nodded once, and I led her away, hiding her embarrassment.

We pushed through the silk curtains, and behind us, the boos faded as the scene ended. Feet shifted as patrons stood to go to the bathroom or the bar; many left. The curtain hid a dark backstage area just wide enough for two of the girls to walk side by side. By the door leading to the changing room was a rack of outfits. Light shone from beneath the threshold. For Midnight and I, as big as we were, we barely fit. I took a step back, gave her space.

She adjusted her outfit and hid her wardrobe malfunction with a few sniffles.

"Thanks," She whispered. Her voice shook.

"You good?"

"Can you ask one of the other girls to cover my show... I need a drink."

"Want me to bring you something?"

"I'll get it."

74

Her arms hugged the jacket taut around her chest, and she wandered away, down the aisle behind the stage until she emerged in the dim light of the lounge close to the bar. A few of the patrons glanced at her, the bright scarlet jacket and skirt now a flat red without the gleam of the stage lights. The glitter on her face had not run, despite her tears, but the light reflecting off each sparkling mote shone different where the tears still dampened her cheeks.

It was the first time Midnight ever left the stage mid-show. It was the first time I'd ever heard someone boo her.

Behind the backstage, the changing area formed a small, stark chamber lined with brightly lit make-up mirrors and tables bearing each girl's tools of the trade. On the far wall, by the fire escape, was a row of lockers where they stored their personal belongings during the shift. Most were backpacks full of school work. One woman brought her diaper bag with her, in case she needed to rush home to take care of her son. It was hard imagining their lives outside of the make-up, the glitter, the skimpy outfits.

Chantel sat at her table, fixing her hair after her private dance. When she saw me enter, she held up the brush.

"Mind running it through a few times in the back?"

I accepted the brush and did as she asked: this was normal. The bar didn't have much of a crew to handle small things, so the bouncer often ended up helping with small tasks as needed. In the months I'd been here, I'd learned to apply lipstick, mascara, and braid hair into pigtails. The girls giggled and said it was good to know in case I ever had a daughter of my own. I was glad my skin was so dark; they never knew when I was blushing.

"You busy after this?" I asked.

"No, that was my last client til the end of my shift. What's going out there? I heard booing."

The brush untangled silky locks. Chantel's hair was so long she always needed help. At the bottom of the curtain of hair, she had a few split ends. They'd taught me to spot that too; let them know when I did.

"Midnight had a wardrobe malfunction."

Chantel glanced back, "Did it...?"

"You knew?" I asked.

She shrugged; her hair bounced and spilled around to her front. I never touched the girls hair with my hands, even though most probably wouldn't complain. It felt a step too far, too affectionate.

"Of course. All the girls knew."

I pursed my lips, "Can you cover her show?"

Before she replied, a shout echoed from the lounge, followed by a scream. I dropped the brush and ran out, and Chantel was halfway out of her chair. The girls rarely intervened, but sometimes, they followed to pull the girl away while I dealt with the customer.

I shoved aside the curtain and saw Midnight at the bar with a tall glass of alcohol, something bright and fruit, the same color as her outfit. The girls rarely drank on shift, but nobody blamed her if she needed one to calm her nerves tonight. Unfortunately, she wasn't alone at the bar. Chantel's weasel leaned on the bar beside her. His pale cheeks were flushed with liquor and excitement, and his thin hair stuck up on the sides from his time with Chantel. As soon as I entered the room, the crowd watching the exchange parted to let me pace, and I stomped my way towards the bar.

"Come on, you can tell me: what's your real name?" Weasel grinned. His lips were slick with spittle or booze or both. The collar of his shirt was popped on the left side, half his buttons undone revealing a scrawny man with skin paler than Midnight's. She leaned away from him.

"Please just leave me alone, sir.'

His hand reached out towards her chest, "Are they real?"

She swatted his hand away, and his lips opened, a strand of saliva connecting the two. His tongue flicked out to swallow it back as his face contorted into anger—the same anger he'd had when I didn't answer his question earlier that day. The bartender saw me coming and waved me over.

"Just let me give them a touch," He hissed, "I'll pay you for it..."

"I'm off shift. Please, leave me—"

The man's hand shoved past her arms to grab her chest, but I lunged forward and shoved the man off his stool. He tumbled to the ground in a heap of limp limbs. His eyes glazed over, and he took a moment to realize where he was and why the ceiling was in front of him instead of Midnight. As he came back to, his cheeks turned red as Midnight's jacket.

"How dare you touch me!"

"Sir, I have to ask you to leave."

"You can't do this to me! I'm a paying customer!"

"We reserve the right to refuse to serve any customer at any time. Please leave before we have to call the police."

His finger came up, shaking with rage, "That tranny started it!"

Behind me, Midnight turned towards the bar and hid her face. The crowd murmured, and those closest weren't saying anything nice. The bartender's jaw locked up, and he put a hand on Midnight's shoulder. At the back of the room, Chantel peeked out of the curtains.

Without thinking, I wrapped my hand around the man's arm and lifted him up, off the ground, off his feet. He hung in the air, feet inches off the ground. I lifted him up until I stared him in the eye. Suddenly, he was swaying in the air, feet kicking at my knees.

"Get out," I growled.

He deflated, hanging limp in my arm as the flush faded from his checks, replaced with a terrified pale. I let his arm go, and he collapsed to the ground again. He crawled backwards a few steps, away from me, before scrambling to his feet. He spared Midnight a glance, but I took a single step forward, and he dashed for the door. As it swung closed, a few patrons applauded drunkenly before returning to their drinks and snacks.

I let out an angry breath and turned to the bar. Midnight stared at the door. Through the glass, we watched Weasel stumble into the darkness.

"Thank you," She said quietly.

"I'm just doing my job. Why don't you take the night off? I'll let the boss know what happened."

Behind us, the stage lights came on to reveal Chantel in a sparkly one piece sauntering across the stage. All the attention pulled away from Midnight and I; The bartender shifted to the end of the bar to clean empty glasses.

She reached out with a shaking hand, "Thanks. Would you walk me to my car, Trevion?"

The twang of a Spanish guitar rang in the air as Chantel's dance mingled with a Salsa. She wasn't even hispanic, even if she looked it. The crowd cheered.

"Sure," I took her hand as the Midnight Show began.

Charles Venable is a storyteller from the Southeastern United States with a love of nature and a passion for writing. He believes stories and poems are about getting there, not being there, and he enjoys those tales that take their time getting to the point.

Rick, the Drummer is No More
Alan Kennedy

Could my remaining cornea become detached during a strenuous sex session? The doctor smirks, lovemaking is always good for you. At my favourite lakeside spot on the way home, I make out the sound check at the jazz club, where a memorial concert for the resident band's drummer will be held at twelve this evening. Rick, the pumping heart, the pulsing soul, a candle through the dark manuscript. Rick, a monosyllabic name to suit his conversational style, a bass drum kick name, not like Jerome the pianist or the double bass player, Bartholomew. Rick, the drummer whose Atlas-like shoulders sustained the band, is no more.

My scream skimmed across the water startling three herons stalking their salamanders. No, not the drummer! It should never have ended up like this! Until Rosie changed the CD, took her attention off the road and with it one of my eyes and my left arm, I was the A-list skin beater, a top-notch musician. Tomorrow, her cast comes off, we take her motorised wheelchair back next Friday, she'll be walking soon. Lucky her.

Rick, my best student, took over.

The cornea is hanging on by its fingertips. If I close my right eye, I can't see the car in front of me, never mind its licence plate. Until the other one follows suit which it will, I'll keep on driving. My coordination is all to pot. I bump into walls, trip over the carpet, I can't judge distances like before. It's a matter of time before they take my licence away.

My studio was my escape, my only relief, the only time I'm not angry at Rosie, apart from in the club the first Friday of every month. I heard her shout from her wheelchair downstairs. (The stair lift is on the to-do list, number fourteen of thirteen items.) The police pulled over one of the band and shot him while he was reaching for his papers. Straight away, I knew it was not the thin-faced anaemic keyboard player or the double bass player who was a white policeman's son.

Not the drummer, not... the... drummer. Please not him. Not my Rick. Maybe the stuck-up pianist who cold-shoulders the public, definitely the double bass player who no one listens to anyway. But not the drummer. His shiny muscles, his cheeky grin, not the bassists constipated expression, or the freckled pianist's furrowed frown. My housebound routine revolves around him.

If the drummer is gone, bang goes our life. He was in intensive care for two weeks, before they switched his life support off. No insurance. My car wouldn't start when I was on my way to pay it myself. Before the taxi arrived, they had already unplugged him.

I can't hit a barn door never mind a tom. My daughter wants me to stop driving even knowing my car is my life, going to out of the way places. The fact you can't get there on the bus is a plus for me. To have an invalid's travel pass means death.

Now an anonymous drummer, a face I can't make out,slaves over the snare drum at the sound check, different strokes, not for me folks. Never again will I listen to jazz, nor to the constant moaning, the bickering of my guilt-driven wife.

I have yet to notice the strengthening of other senses. I can hear better if I see the person's lips, yet my hearing is going with age. I always put the English subtitles on in the DVDs. I nearly bought a white cane, a beautiful one with an ivory handle and a whistle activated location device should I put it down.

With the dimming light, the lake's corrugated surface reminds me of drying custard. Mallard ducks with their diamond white on black heads compete with a peewit forcing out its last wit. The unseasonal cold weather does not deter a young couple cuddling in winter clothing under the still leafless trees. A faint white circle of sun tries to prise its way through the black clouds. The clinking of someone playing a local tune on the accordion mixes with distant cowbells on real cows. By the sounds of it, a murder of crows have found something tasty. Rain still doesn't fall.

I was Rick's guide; he was me, an extension of me. Hearing him drum was like listening to myself, the same high-hat patterns, the same intense bass drum kicks propelling the song in a multi-rhythmic groove. Now he's gone. I can't listen to a replacement. Part of my enjoyment was seeing Rick's face as he thrashed out the complex rhythms. I could feel his gaze;I knew he would be playing only for me.

These memories are a bank to withdraw from whenever I want. All banks are robbers and this one is no different, a bank with no interest, only diminishing returns. My sight is dwindling more and more. I can hardly see my granddaughter's little smile;I can feel it with my fingers and she's still small enough to treat my fumbling like a game.

At the lake, one mallard then another duck under the water looking for worms. The new wooden path to the water's edge is specially designed for wheelchairs. How considerate, how modern. I could bring Rosie here and shove her to a watery grave. These sights will soon vanish forever. What good is my enhanced hearing if I can't listen to my music? The concert starts at eight, I've another twenty minutes to kill. I could murder a pint, drown my sorrows.

My phone goes. It's Rosie. I can't talk to her. I still hear myself warning of the tree zooming up. Still crooked from the crash, the ancient oak beside the lake stoops to cradle me. I throw the tow rope over its stoutest branch. A lovely last view. I'll wait till the band strikes up Rick's favourite tune, Round Midnight. Maybe they'll have a memorial concert for me too. Maybe not.

*Originally from Glasgow, Scotland, **Alan Kennedy** has been living in Spain for the past 27 years. His first degree was in musical composition and he has worked as musical director for theatre, English teacher, grave digger, sales rep and recently (the last 15 years) as a storyteller, travelling round the country for nine months of the year.*

He started writing five years ago whilst training as a creative coach and found that most of his clients were struggling writers. Inventing stories has since become his main creative outlet. Alan Kennedy has one daughter, Charlie, who is on the point of finishing Medical school. Apart from the creative arts, Alan's other passions include yoga, snorkelling, cooking and learning languages. He is currently studying Basque, his partner's mother tongue.

On the Lookout for Bo
Kimberly Stammen

There was a new trawler in harbor. A battered, scuffed-red hulk with a look about her as if she'd just barely made it to dock, and wasn't in any hurry to go out again. I don't know much about boats, despite riding the harbor path past them nearly every day for six years, but even I could see that the deck was none too clean, the fishing rod stirrups inexpertly mended with scrap wood and duct tape, and the whole thing seemed, just slightly, to list.

I swung a leg off my bike, flipped the stand, and stepped out on the dock. It was a still afternoon, early summer, and the water glassily reflected the crisp white or primary colors of the other fresh-washed vessels. The scarred trawler was as out of place as a rock in an egg carton. Walking round to its stern, I read the name "'Round Midnight," in letters so worn they were nearly gone. Suddenly the cabin door burst open,and jazz music poured out. Along with the music came a wizened specimen, a pipe protruding from his grizzled beard, old clothes dripping off him like seaweed. He looked at me with the piercing light eyes of either the true fisherman or the fanatic--if there was a difference--and said, "It's Monk, missy, listen!"

No one before or since has called me anything as incongruous as missy and lived to talk about it. But something about the old guy made me forgive the salutation, and besides,he was right, it was the great and idiosyncratic pianist splashing through his little tin speakers.I said, "Sure."

My dad used to play all the jazz piano greats for me, late at night when I couldn't practice any more but also couldn't sleep. He said the jazz would balance out all that Beethoven stuck in my head. Maybe he'd been right; since he died I hadn't listened to anything except myself playing the classical pieces I had to learn, and my head certainly wasn't in balance. The old guy cocked his head at me, spit over the side, and with a wise intuition belied by literally everything that surrounded him, asked,"you play?"

He didn't seem freaked or awkward, which is how people usually are when they talk to me. Perhaps it's my Harley,or the bandana I habitually wear. Perhaps it's just that I'm big, and so tall I look over people's heads,while they, I suppose, look straight into my boobs, which have been called imposing. Perhaps it's my nose ring, or that I never say much. But probably what freaks people out most, even in this town that my dad loved for its equanimity as much as for its gentle harbor at the wild gnashing mouth of the Columbia River, is the usual: I'm a classical pianist. People don't get that, and what they don't get scares them. They gush or run. So, like cancer or serious money, it's something I mostly don't mention.

But this guy seemed harmless. "Yeah," I answered.

Right away I knew I was in for it. His eyes lit up and his eyebrows furred out, and he leaped up and pounced into the clutter behind him, muttering. The crazy old coot played viola, apparently. He had one stashed in the bow, next to some tackle and line and antique Japanese buoys. When he reappeared, a few moments later--after some crashing--with an instrument case more battered than his boat, his fingers were trembling with excitement. I had to get out of there.

"Sorry, old man," I said. "My shift starts in a minute."

He completely ignored me. He opened the case and lifted up the viola. He showed me the bow and bragged how he had gotten it in a junk store, "and it's worth more than my boat, missy!" I smiled because of how little that said, and realized I was beginning to enjoy him. I'd spent most of my life pursuing unattainable perfection in music; since my dad died I had forgotten completely that there was such a thing as enjoyment.

"If Monk played a string instrument, it would have been viola," said the old coot, deep into his monomania now. "So I got one, and when nothing's biting and the old girl's not taking on water,"--he patted the gunwale--"I'm learning to play."He gestured for me to come aboard, and started sawing.

I really was going to be late for my dish washing shift at Wangs,the local terrible Chinese place. This town clings to the juncture of the Columbia and the Pacific like a barnacle, barely subsisting on fishing charters, crabbing, and summer tourists. There aren't many jobs, certainly no other boss like Wang, who lets me take four months off every autumn to solo with orchestras in NYC and Europe and never says one word about it. The restaurant's food really is terrible--possibly because Wang himself is the only person of Chinese heritage within twenty miles, and he isn't a cook--and my agent clamors for me to move somewhere more convenient, more sensible, so I can perform all year round and not have to ruin my hands doing what she calls "normal shit work." But dish washing, like anonymity, seems to help keep me from floundering.

The little man scratched his bow over the strings with such ridiculous and endearing concentration, in total opposition to the tunes still pouring from some hidden radio, that despite the risk to my job, I shrugged and stepped aboard. Felt my weight rock the craft. I shook my head at myself, wondering what I was doing, and stepped gingerly through the collection of detritus littering the stern: a tarnished samovar, a pile of crab pots, something that looked like part of a spinning wheel. The sound of the viola bristled against the calm air and the order of the other boats,which were hosed down after the days' work, their ropes coiled, gear stowed. One of the mysteries of life, I thought, was why viola attracts the oddities of personality; the iconoclasts, the misfits, the egocentrics and solipsists, those attracted and satisfied by the possibility and often the necessity of unremitting toil and unheralded splendor. Those who search out the obscure, the difficult, the frankly crazy, and proudly call themselves quixotics,whether tilting bows in the middle of orchestras or oceans.

I found a rickety deck chair, and sank into it. "You go out all by yourself? Out past the breakers?" I was either skeptical or deeply impressed. I imagining being two miles out, on the fickle calm of deep ocean, the closest boats mere dots on the horizon. The sting of salt air, the smell of diesel, the sun's glare blinding, the world beneath my feet tilting and rocking. Playing whatever I thought the salmon and seagulls might want to hear.

"And you, missy?" he asked. "What's your instrument?"

I don't know what I was thinking--I suppose I was entranced by the impossibility of pianists performing for fishies--but I told him and he practically fell off his chair. He was enraged! His craggy cheeks and his hooked nose--the only parts of his face not hidden by beard--reddened like a steamed crab. "Do you mean to tell me," he spluttered, "there's a world class musician right here in this town? Right now on this boat?" He stood up, he started yelling and jumping around, waving the bow like a mad maestro's baton. People started poking their heads out of the neat, level trawlers and pleasure boats lined up down the dock. "Why doesn't everyone in town know it?" he yelled. "I'm going to tell them! Hey! Hey!"

And then my cell rang; it was Wang phoning to say, "you so late why!"

I begged the excited old coot, whose name turned out to be Bo, to keep his mouth shut. After much hurried pleading, I ended up having to agree--even as I was dashing off the dock, kicking up the stand, revving up and putting in gear— to come back after my shift for a brew, his treat. Despite the near panic his inclination to tell everyone how great I was put me into, I was shaking my head and grinning at the same time as I tore out of there. I'd agreed to come back to mollify the old guy,but what the heck? Beethoven never offered me a beer.

Drinking with Bo turned out to be a fairly regular thing that summer. After my usual four or five hours of practice I'd ride the harbor path every afternoon, to town for errands and then to Wang's for work. Whenever I saw the 'Round Midnight tied up, which was as often as a few times a week, I'd head down there after my shift. We'd have beers, look at the stars. He'd say I was hiding my light under a bushel; I'd say "yeah yeah can it old man." He'd come up with various outrageous plans: to get me invited to the town's summer music festival, to do evening jams on sticky bar pianos,to play for Sunday school classes, to get an interview on local radio;I'd calmly explain all the reasons I categorically refused to be known. He was incorrigible, he was obtuse. He continually thought up ideas that threatened, not only my anonymity, but the rest I needed from the monumental stress of preparing for, and recovering from, the months on tour, and most importantly my precariously-balanced symbiotic co-existence with the town. The town that, without knowing or caring, was my only home.

But he amused me, and I thought I could keep his mouth shut with reminders and beer.

"Why are you even here?" he asked one evening. It was August, I would leave in a less than a month, and my stress was mounting. I gritted my teeth.

"Why are you?" I responded, defiant. I'd often wondered who he really was, or had been, before he stepped on the 'Round Midnight. But I was trying to get him to keep my life secret; it hadn't seemed balanced to inquire about his.

He wasn't having it. "In this particular town. Why?"

I narrowed my eyes at him, sipped my beer. He was a good enough guy. More than that, he was a mystery, like me. Fleeing something, looking for something, getting the two goals mixed up. I decided I owed him a try.

"My dad died here," I said. I told him my mom died before I could remember anything about her, and my dad raised me, working long hours every day at a big city job. "He got me the best teachers, he took me to lessons, he wangled concert tickets and the tuition for expensive summer chamber music camps. Since he first heard me play, when I was, like, maybe three, he knew, he told me later. So he worked, and he saved, and finally he bought me a fucking Steinway. He wasn't the one who taught me how to use it, but he was still the one who taught me what to use it for."

My voice broke. In the ensuing silence even the boat stopped rocking and listing. I went on."When I went to Eastman, full scholarship, he thought I was set. He retired from the job I guess he hated, bought a small house and moved clear across the country to here." I'd never heard him mention Ilwaco before he capsized his life and started anew. "We'd talk on the phone. He told me about the boats and the sun rises, about how they shut up the Merri-go-round after Labor Day. How a Merri-go-round looks when it's all closed up in the winter,the rain pelting it. He liked seeing things when they were closed for the season. When they weren't intended to be seen, when they weren't on the stage."

I popped another beer, leaned back in the spindly, debatable chair. The grey-black sky hid all but the most insistent stars. Every time my performances approached, the same contradictory emotions roiled me: the pitch of exultation and power at being on a stage;the slanting plunge into terror at those very same things.

"I was planning my debut recital at Carnegie Hall. I talked to dad nearly every day, between rehearsing arranging things and arguing with my agent and all of that. Dad kept me sane. He thought we were just talking about walking the boardwalk, or when the fish bite best. Of course, he planned to come for the recital," I said. And my voice broke again, and this time I did stop.

Bo, the viola already in his lap, started sawing. It took me a while, through the maze of his mistakes and bad pitch, to realize the tune he was trying to play was 'Round Midnight. It's a difficult tune, a melody that leaps upwards in unpredictable intervals, with wide spaces between gestures where the rhythm can sag. The sound of it was so bad that it transcended into something past sound, past bebop or avant guarde, and into ethereality. I shook my head, but, as always with Bo, felt the tug at the corner of my mouth, the small smile.

"I walked out onstage," my voice was a murmur barely registering above the strange music. "And I saw all those faces looking up at me before the lights dimmed, and I knew he wasn't there." I didn't say it was the worst moment of my life, because it was supposed to be the best. I didn't say how long I sat, with all those unseen eyes glaring, adjusting to the knowledge--gained from the steadiness he had shown me all my life--that if he wasn't there he was dead. I was unmoored. And that even so he would want me to do what I loved, and to play.

"Well shit, missy," said Bo softly, as he continued to saw.

I left for my tour of Sweden, Finland, and Norway,doing Beethoven Concertos numbers 1,2, and 4.I'd also prepared a recital of Scriabin--another fine nutty old coot--and some stuff by contemporary Nordic composers. When I got back to Ilwaco I went down to the docks. I didn't see the 'Round Midnight, and none of the fishermen knew where Bo was.

"That guy," said one.

"I think he's part leprechaun," said another.

I resumed my shift at Wang's, and every afternoon rode slow past the harbor, my bike protesting, checking for Bo. I'd asked my agent to see if she could get me in at the town's summer music festival;I was nervous about it, and wanted the reassurance of his triumphant bow waving in the air.

I'm still looking out for him; he could be anywhere, anywhere in the world or under it. I'll let you know when I see him again.

Kimm Brockett Stammen's *writings have appeared or are forthcoming in Typehouse, Rosebud Magazine, Crack the Spine Anthology, Atticus Review, Adelaide, Meat for Tea: The Valley Review, and others. She was a 2nd Place winner in Typehouse Magazine's 2019 short fiction contest. She received an MFA in Creative Writing from Spalding University in Louisville, KY.*
Before beginning work on her MFA at Spalding University, Kimm was a concert saxophonist, clinician and music instructor. She now lives in Seattle, WA, in a century-old house, with her husband of 30-some years. They have an awesome daughter in college, and a perpetually muddy dog named Birdie.

Katy's Penance
David Mackinnon

Fire raged as the screams of lost souls shrieked through the smoke and flames into the dark of night.

Katy lay back on the soft cold grass - a hundred or so meters from the blaze. The heat of the fire flushed her cheeks and the stars that had winked their luminescent eyes at the moon only a few moments ago, were now obscured by the billowing smoke, as the remnants of the village hall turned to flame and then ash.

Katy closed her eyes to the carnage before her and one question burned in her mind;

"What the fuck just happened?!?"

Katy strained to see through the windscreen of her old Fiat. Thick fog enveloped the little car and obscured any help she might have had from the haunting brightness of the full moon that loomed above her not long ago.

The fog had quickly surrounded her as she had driven as fast as she could from the wreck of her life - her former life! And she was now unsure as to exactly where she was.

It was late, she was tired and just needed to find somewhere to stop for the night; get some sleep and then push on to somewhere, anywhere.

Then, as suddenly as it had appeared, the fog lifted and the moon was back, its sinister gaze lighting the road ahead.

In the near distance, she could just make out the black silhouettes of houses.

'Yes' she thought. 'A village! There's bound to be a hotel or B&B'

Katy's hopes were buoyed as she drove into the little village to look for somewhere to stay. So relieved was she, to find civilisation out here in the middle of no-where, that she did not see the sign welcoming her.

On the roadside, obscured by the thorny claws of the hedgerow that had grown over its surface, was an ancient wooden stake, hammered deep into the ground and decayed from age. Upon this stake was a wooden plaque, nailed into place with jagged looking, rusty nails, their sharp tips protruding as if from the end of a mace. This plaque bore the town's name, blood red slashes carved painfully into its wooden flesh.

Midnight, it read. Visitors Welcome!

The town seemed to be just like all the towns around here. A high street, an old marketplace, and lots of Tudor buildings.

Katy spotted a B&B almost straight away and pulled into the small carpark round the back. It was pitch black, there were no streetlamps and the B&B had no outside lighting.

'Probably don't get many visitors at this time', she thought.

Katy stepped out of her car and braced herself for waking up the landlord and the inevitable awkward conversation that would follow.

The darkness seemed to shroud her as she shut the car door and once the sound of it slamming had faded, the darkness was filled with almost complete silence. The only sound that leached itself through the black of the night was the creak and groan of huge trees that lined the back of the car park.

'Strange,' she thought, 'There was no wind at all.'

Walking carefully, she made her way to the front door of the B&B. It was slow progress as she could barely see where she was putting her feet, and the full moon that had so ably lit the road into town earlier, just hung there, mocking her from above.

Eventually, she reached the front door and knocked loud and clear.

Katy was running through a story in her head. One that would convince whoever answered the door that she was, in fact, a normal young lady with a perfectly rational reason for banging on their door at this late hour.

A bolt slammed back so suddenly that Katy nearly jumped in the air.

Then another.

She took a deep breath.

The handle of the door slowly turned, emitting a painful screech that seemed to cut right through Katy's head like an electrically charged hatchet. She winced and as the sound stopped, Katy noticed that the moon was now shining its pallid yellow glow on the door.

It opened just enough for the long, gaunt face of a man to peer out.

"Yes?" said a deep, rumbling baritone. "How may I help you?"

"Ah, yes well my name is Katy…"

"Of course, it is." He interrupted; his tone blank.

"Um, yup, well I was travelling from a friend's house and just seemed to lose track of time… and… well, then I realised it was late and that I had better find somewhere to stay for the night?"

This last line was finished on a high note, leaving an unasked question hanging between them like a bandit in the gallows.

The man nodded solemnly, opening the door and beckoning her inside.

He was a tall, slim man, stooped with age so that his head was almost level with Katy's. His eyes were sunken deep into his head and dark shadows shrouded them from her view. Despite his size and age, he moved with quick, silent movements and managed the door with ease even though it seemed to be thick oak with heavy looking hinges and bolts.

The hair on his head was thin and white. Only now did Katy notice that he was fully dressed in an old-fashioned, black, three-piece suit, complete with black tie.

'Jeez,' Katy thought, 'perhaps he sleeps in it?'

As if reading her mind, he said, "I have just returned from a funeral. It went on longer than expected. Otherwise, I would have retired to bed a long time ago. I only have one room available, in the back on the ground floor. You can have that if you like?"

"That would be great."

There were no lights and a candle burned on a small reception desk just inside the door, the air was frigid.

"Candles? Have you had a power cut?"

"No, I like to use candles. They are more environmentally friendly, are they not?"

"Erm yeah, I guess they are. It gets dark around here doesn't it?" said Katy shivering.

"Well, this is Midnight." He said, opening a small cupboard and retrieving a key.

Katy puzzled at his choice of words.

'This is midnight.?? Surely he meant it is midnight?'

She thought about correcting him when he spoke again.

"I am sorry about the cold. This is an old house and can become as frigid as a morgue at night."

Again, the strange choice of words jarred with Katy, but she was tired and put it down to lack of sleep.

She took the key and almost gasped at the coldness of his touch. Katy jerked her hand back, immediately embarrassed.

"Bad circulation!" He offered, "One of the pit-falls of my age."

"Oh, I'm sorry. Do you need me to sign anything?"

"That will not be necessary until morning."

"Ok, well my name is Katy...."

"I am Jacob, Jacob Pyre. Pleased to meet you Katy Morgan."

He turned and took Katy through a door to the left of the desk and down a narrow corridor. At the end of the corridor, there was a hall with two doors. He motioned to the one on the left and bid Katy goodnight.

Katy closed the door, a candle already burned on the bedside table.

An urge to lock the door swept over her and Katy gave in to it. As she did, a scary thought came to her.

'How did he know my surname??' She thought. 'Did I say it without realising? I am very tired.'

Katy decided the best thing to do was to crawl under the sheets and let sleep take her. All would seem different in the morning; she was sure of that.

Katy awoke with a start, an ice-cold hand gently but urgently shaking her.

She sat bolt upright, still wearing last night's clothes.

"Miss Morgan, we must evacuate immediately." Said Jacob Pyre, his voice bland and deep, offering no alarm.

As Katy's eyes focused, she could see that it was still dark outside.

'What time is it?' She thought.

"What? What's happened?" she asked groggily.

"I will explain on the way, but now you must ready yourself, quickly. I will be waiting outside your room."

And with that he turned and left.

Katy threw the covers back. The cold was bracing, and she wrapped her coat tight around her shoulders.

Jacob stood motionless outside her door, the dull glow of a candle illuminating his long stern face. It looked luminescent, like a full moon, glowing and creepy.

They left the B&B as Jacob explained about a gas leak in town. They had been 'advised' to gather in the town hall on the opposite side of the town and a safe distance from the leak.

Katy was still groggy and didn't even notice that the streets were still deserted. She blindly followed Jacob Pyre down the pitch-black high street to the town hall, where everyone was gathering.

Where she would be safe.

Suddenly, the town hall came into view. It was white and, just like Jacob's face, seemed to glow against the black canvas of night.

'It's quite hypnotic,' Katy thought.

Jacob pushed the huge double doors of the building and they glided smoothly open, revealing a large hall with rows and rows of bench seats, all facing the opposite wall where there was a lectern.

Standing at the lectern was a woman. She smiled as they entered and raised her hands in a gesture of welcome. But there was nothing welcoming about this woman. She was skeletal in appearance and when she smiled, it looked as if her head might split in two. Her white hair was pulled tightly back into a ponytail and her skin was virtually transparent, displaying a network of pulsing veins. Even this, however, could not distract from her dull yellow teeth, and what terrible teeth they were.

They jutted, shark-like, from her gums; ragged, razor-sharp shards.

Her long, clawed fingers gripped the sides of the lectern.

"Welcome, Jacob. I see you have brought a new guest for us to meet."

"Yes, Lady Eve. She arrived not long ago. I thought you would like to welcome her to town."

Only then, did Katy drag her eyes from this hideous woman and cast her eyes around.

The room was lit with flaming torches, and there were candles running up the walkway that split the benches down the middle.

On the benches, watching her with their own terrible smiles were 20 more ghoulish residents.

She turned and tried to flee but the strong, cold hands of Jacob Pyre gripped her like a vice.

"Do not worry Katy Morgan, this will all be over soon." He said

And for the first time Katy saw a flicker of emotion on his face. Relief, maybe? Then no sooner had it appeared than it had gone.

Jacob spun her around and tied her hands with thick rope.

"No point in struggling Katy; the ropes will not come free by your hand."

She looked at him, fury and fear contorting her features and, there it was again. The pallid, emotionless mask slipped for a moment. And while Lady Eve had turned to retrieve something, Jacob winked at her and subtly loosened the knot so that the rope still hung around her hands, but Katy was as free as a bird.

Then, with extraordinary strength, Jacob lifted her by the arms and calmly carried her, still upright, to where the lectern was. He placed her there, between two torches mounted at head height. Katy stood rooted to the spot with fear, as Lady Eve approached her. She moved slowly, as if stalking prey and a hungry look filled her face as her tongue flicked over rapier teeth like a snake tasting the air.

She reached out with one of her clawed fingers and gently caressed Katy's cheek, she flinched but could not find the courage to move, and a shudder of pleasure rattled the monster before her.

Lady Eve shook her head to clear it and turned to the others. A thought appeared in Katy's head, like a bolt of lightning!

'Grab the torch!'

'Grab the torch and stab her!'

'Stab her right in the back! '

'Through to her black heart.'

And so, with a feeling that she was not entirely in control of her own body, she shed the ropes from her hands and reached up to the flaming torch on her right. Then, Katy calmly braced her feet against the floor before thrusting the burning stake into the back of this 'thing' in front of her.

There was a dull thud as it hit Lady Eve and then it seemed to go deep into her back with relative ease.

Then the scream! It was the most wicked and unholy sound she had ever heard, and with it, Lady Eve caught fire. In fact, she lit up as if she had petrol in her veins.

Her eyes exploded, mini fireballs erupting from the sockets as she staggered, now engulfed with fire, into the crowd of shocked looking spectators.

As she grasped at each one of her congregation, they too became engulfed in flames, their screams loud above the roar of fire.

At the opposite end of the hall, Jacob Pyre watched, a smile dancing along his lips. He turned and left, locking the doors from the outside.

The fire grew in intensity and despite her terror driven efforts, Katy was forced to the back of the hall where she found a small door. She ran, coughing and spluttering from the smoke and threw herself against it grasping for the handle. The door gave way and Katy stumbled into the night, eyes streaming from smoke and sheer, overwhelming emotion.

Katy awoke with a start; she lay where she had dropped after escaping the inferno and looked across to what was left of the old building. Smouldering remains were all she could see, and she wondered how long she had been out for.

Then a voice drifted to her from the darkness.

"Katy."

"Jacob?" she replied

"Yes Katy, it is Jacob Pyre. I really do hope you are not badly hurt."

"No, I mean, I don't think so. What the fuck just happened?!?" she croaked.

"I think it would be best if you were to accompany me back to the guest house and have a good rest before I explain everything. Will you do that Katy? Will you sleep and wait till morning before you leave? I can explain what I know later."

"Erm, yes ok. I definitely need some sleep. I am so tired."

Jacob Pyre helped Katy to her feet and helped her back down the high street to his guest house.

'Just till morning.' He thought. 'Although round midnight, morning never comes.'

And once again, he smiled.

Undisclosed Desires
Efi P.

It smells so good!

She shouted out loud. Her voice echoed in the empty attic.

Holding tight a bouquet of yellow tulips, she made a dance pose and accidentally slipped on the floor. She couldn't help it and burst out laughing.

In the oldest standing mansion of the province, owned by the family Van Dijk the year's closing celebration was underway.

Mr and Mrs Van Dijk welcomed their business partners and family members in their spectacular sitting room. A gold-lined sofa and a drinks table were set up in the corner of the room.

Thick curtains were covering the floor-to-ceiling windows whereon the shadows of the figures dancing in the room appeared to be taller than in real.

The frolicking candle flames created a shadow dance on the high ceilings while the guests were enjoying themselves toasting with a glass of champagne or a Chateau Latour.

Descendants of the Dutch royal family, Van Dijk, had two children. Sammi was the youngest, an eleven years old boy and his older sister was now 18. Her name was Serene.

Untouched by the sun, Serene and her brother were growing up in a very strict household.

Serene was going through struggles in her childhood. Her religious upbringing made her feel guilty for her sexuality and ashamed of her cheerful character.

Now, in her puberty, she tried her parent's patience. At first, she refused to go to the church every Sunday with her parents. Mr and Mrs Van Dijk had to warn her a few times. If she wouldn't change her behavior the planned winter skiing holidays in Bern would be cancelled.

Serene loved skiing. She loved the freedom while sliding on snow and the speed when skiing downhill. Her urge to challenge the tight boundaries of her parents' fears and exceed the limits of normality was growing lately faster than she could handle.

On the contrary, her youngest brother was treated like a little king. Sammi was free to do everything he wanted. He was intelligent and loved mathematics and physics. After a few failed experiments at home, his parents decided to hire a teacher to guide him.

Two months ago, a rainy autumn day, the doorbell rang. A young man walked into the hallway. His footsteps made no sound, and they sank gently into the Persian carpet.

"I am Daniel. Pleased to meet you Sir and Madam and thank you for the invitation. It is an honor to be here".

"We are very delighted to welcome you to our home, Mr Goldsmith. An esteemed scientist as you is the ideal teacher for Sammi". Mr Van Dijk said while greeting him with a handshake.

"As we hear you are unfamiliar to the surroundings. May I ask what brings you in the Netherlands?" "Certainly Mr Van Dijk. A young scientist as me is looking for challenges and the Netherlands offers a lot! The water science here is exemplary! I am just about to start with some research and development needs in irrigation. Afterwards, I will go back to my small hometown in Ohio where my home is. My father is a farmer, growing soybeans and corn. We are living in a big farmhouse, as big as this house is but...less luxurious I guess.." Daniel said hesitantly.

Mrs Van Dijk`s eyes shined. She knew that the young man had a lot of skills, after all, Dr.Otker had recommended him. But now she could tell how charming he was.

His body was full, large and wide and his hands looked strong. Obviously, he got the benefits of the farming workout when helping his father.

His dark bruin hair was just above his shoulders, in a messy play with his delicate facial futures. His lips were full and his eyes, deep green with narrowed eyebrows were staring now at the corridor.

"How is life in the United States Mr. Goldsmith?" Mrs Van Dijk asked in a friendly tone.

The heavy thump of footsteps on the stairs interrupted their conversation.
Serene was almost gliding down the stairs while singing: "Such a beautiful day, for getting away...". Her voice faded out when she realized that her parents and a stranger were downstairs, staring at her.

Daniel glanced timidly at her and lowered quickly his eyes while his heart was going like mad.

That song, he wished he could forget. He couldn`t. It was impossible after what had happened to her. Her death shook him to the core. She was his first and only love. His heart pulse was going very fast, his head went dizzy. His flashback interrupted Mrs Van Dijk`s voice.

"Serene, we have a guest," she said, gravely.

"Mr Goldsmith is here to teach Sammi physics and mathematics. He will stay with us a couple of months, aren`t you Daniel?" Mr Van Dijk geared towards Daniel shifting his mental state.

"Ahh, yes, I suppose." his voice cracked. His forehead was sweaty and his strong hands were shaking, attesting his restlessness.

Serene looked at him. She could smell from distance his perfume. His light bruin skin was glistening with sweat. His awkwardness seemed to amuse her. She gained her temperament back and arrogantly greeted him.

"Welcome Mr Goldsmith, I am Serene".

Her dress almost slipped off her shoulders revealing her beautiful breasts. She pulled her dress up and turned to her mother.

"Sissi is asking if I can help her fixing her dress for the Proms. Can I go out now?"

"I am afraid you cannot. Sammi will be here soon and I would like us to have altogether lunch with Mr Goldsmith".

"Serene, please go now, we must finish our talk with Daniel. We will call you downstairs once Sammi is back" Mr Van Dijk said.

Serene didn`t reply. Upset as she was, turned immediately her back and climbed up the stairs while singing in a sarcastically tone: "Such a beautiful day, for getting away..."

Daniel could hardly function. The housemaid served them an hors d'oeuvre and Mr and Mrs Van Dijk welcomed him to take a look at their drawing room.

Their outstanding taste in antiques and fine art caught his attention. The exemplary quality of all artworks in the room impressed Daniel. Last ten years he invested in studying, almost ignoring life`s human-made beauties.

Besides his dedication to science, Daniel was bitten by the archery bug. At the weekends, he used to play with his impressive and very technical compound bow. There he had met her, into the woods. During his scheduled training, he heard a beautiful voice, singing. That song...

"What is your favorite form of art Mr Goldsmith?" Mrs Van Dijk asked.

"I must admit that is difficult for me to select. I like portraits, just like this one!" He pointed to a painting of Johannes Vermeer.

What a brilliant technique! Daniel continued, in a try to share some enthusiasm.

"It is indeed an excellent example of impressionism art Mr Goldsmith" Mrs Van Dijk replied smilingly.

"Now you have to excuse me, I have to check the preparations for lunch. I will see you in the dining room ". She explained and walked away.

Mr Van Dijk walked to his office and Daniel followed him. The two men sat at opposite ends of the table and talked about Daniel`s tasks agreement.

"We expect you to be here for two months. You can stay in the guest room and make use of the teaching room at the end of this corridor", Mr. van Dijk said pointing right with his finger.

"You will work no longer than 6 hours per day and....

Daniel couldn`t hear, no more. His mind was blurry. With a tremulous smile, he asked if he could go to the restroom. The housemaid saw him the way.

"It's all so screamingly boring!" Serene shouted behind a closed door.

Daniel was shaking and stepped quickly into the bathroom, submerging immediately his head in cold water. His heart was beating faster and his thoughts were racing. Her again...and that song. How could she know that song...how could she dare to sing it? Daniel`s hands seemed unable to stay still. He could barely reach the razor from the top of the mirror cabinet.

"Do you need anything Mister?" he heard the housemaid asking.

"What is happening out there?" Serene asked curiously standing now in the open door.

"It`s all fine. Thank you". Daniel answered holding his breath.

Now, two months later, the snow was reflecting the winter sun and the cold air was sliding in from the mansion`s windows. The Scots pine trees and the white-barked birches were standing vulnerable to frost on the actual fence alignment around the mansion walls.

The dinner table was set. A white tablecloth covered the whole table, plates, napkins and glassware were placed carefully and the smell of freshly cooked meat travelled throughout the house. All blue-blooded guests were sitting around the table.

"What a pleasure to have you all here today, this special New Years` eve!" Mrs Van Dijk said while straightening her elegant dress. Next to her was sitting Serene and then her husband. Sammi was next with Daniel following.

"Thank you, dear friends, so much for being here tonight. Daniel, thank you for staying with us these two months. Sammi has definitely learned a lot from you. To science! " Mr Van Dijk said while raising his glass.

"Happiness for everyone!" Daniel toasted with champagne.

"All the best!" Everyone wished the other and kept talking and laughing in the euphoric atmosphere. "Mr Goldsmith", Sammi said, "Tonight I have a strange feeling. Like a bug in my stomach. Do you think something bad is going to happen?".

"Children`s intuition does not lie," said an old woman sitting on their left. Daniel looked at her briefly and bend over to have eye contact with Sammi: "There is nothing to be afraid of. It is just the excitement of the New Year`s Eve. Come on, let`s eat!"

Serene was sitting at the corner of the table, upset and refusing to be part of this cheerful moment.

As the night went on she kept looking angrily at Daniel`s side.

Some weeks before on his first free day in the mansion, Daniel decided to go out. He planned to spend the day wandering among the sand dunes, nearby the mansion. He buttoned up his jacket and put on his hat.

He crossed the big garden and walked out, along the pine trees forest. Their foliage and needleswere dead. Seemed as if they have been sung in a fire. The winter burn had damaged them forevermore.

Daniel heard a whistle. Somebody was whistling a tune he knew. Hastily he began searching around who it might be. Then he saw her. Serene was walking towards him. She darted her eyes into Daniels`. He stared at her. His hands started to sweat and his knees felt weak. Before he could speak out a word she cradled his face and softly kissed him.

He stopped her and pulled her back. His eyes were burning.

"That song...Where do you know this song from?" he screamed.

"I will never let you know. Just to make you wonder" Serene said and shook her hair loose. Her blond hair fell freely upon her naked shoulders.

Daniel went closer. Staring at her eyes, he touched her intimately and smelled her hair.

"It`s a great day for ... getting away!", she sang loudly escaping his touch. She started to run back and Daniel was going after her. Pine foliage blocked her path and soon they found themselves looking at each other, face to face. The wind was blowing strongly and they were heavily breathing when a crash of thunder and a loud cracking sound made them panic.

Suddenly they heard somebody yelling. The voice sound was coming closer and closer.

"Serene, are you there?" It was her father. Mr Van Dijk was searching for her into the woods.

They looked at each other breathless. It felt that the world stood still for a moment.

Back home they never talked about it. In real, Daniel never talked to her again and he was trying to avoid her as much as he could. Up till that night.

After everyone has finished eating, they moved to the living room enjoying their whiskey and cigars.

Mr and Mrs Van Dijk introduced them the two musicians who had just entered the room with their saxophone and cello. Everyone started clapping and the music started. Daniel was accompanying Mr Van Dijk and his friends. It was his last night in the mansion. His bag was waiting ready upstairs and a taxi was planned to pick him up exactly at 11:00 the next morning.

Serene, obviously irritated by his ignorance, kept looking at him angrily while pretending of having fun with her family friends. After a while, round midnight the music stopped. The guests were getting ready for the New year`s countdown.

Suddenly, the gramophone started to play a song: *"It`s a perfect day for getting away.."* Daniel`s eyes narrowed by the sound and seemed to flee from the expanding whites of his eyes.

Serene started to laugh. And she laughed for a while, out loud. He looked at her. His stare was blank. Serene walked out of the room. Daniel did the same. The New Year`s countdown had started. The voices were loud and they could be heard from afar.

Serene walked towards the forest. Daniel followed her into the woods. The air was filled with a putrid odour and the sticky mud made him walk unsteadily. All of a sudden she appeared in front of him. The girl was holding her bow and her long dress was slipping on the wet ground. The girl with the bow was singing that song, her song. The beautiful colourful Northern lights covered the skies. Shivering in the cold, Daniel put his hands in his suit pockets. Searching...

His head was spinning and the girl was now closer in front of him saying: "Don't struggle like that or I will only love you more". Deep red was blurring his eyes and the razor`s edge went through her skin, pulling her skin off her face.

"It can't be you, you are dead". He screamed.

Daniel went back to his room, sweating and without almost a breath.

The morning after, exactly at 11:00 he walked down the stairs holding his bag and a pair of keys.

Mr and Mrs Van Dijk were waiting for him at the front door. Sammi ren out of his room to hug him.

"I will miss you!"

"I will definitely miss you Sammi," said Daniel in a warm tone.

"Mr Goldsmith, this is for the trip," the housemaid said and gave him a bag full of food.

"Very nice of you Clara, I will definitely... Daniel couldn`t finish his sentence and then she appeared. Her long blond hair was shining in the daylight and her eyes darted his.

He stared at her. His hands started to sweat and his knees felt weak...

Cultural Entrepreneur Writer Contemporary Visual Artist Thinker Life Lover
I am a passionate writer and a creative storyteller. Surrealistic & dreamy, symbolic or vivid, my Artworks can reveal depth and power, a necessity or a statement. My full name is Efthymia ¨Cheerfulness" in Greek and nothing makes me more cheerful than making Art. Born and raised in Thessaloniki, Greece the last decade I share my time between Holland, Greece and other attractive destinations in order to explore the world and myself, share inspiration, work and create as a new age nomad. While a continuation of artistic projects were shaping my aesthetics, my social consciousness and my need in making the world a better place activated the seeds of people`s empowerment and the world reshaping through community projects. Producing social awareness events & festivals, my mission is to embrace diversity and create understanding.

Blue Moon
Rae Whitney

Getting around is much easier late at night when most people sleep the sleep of the dead, escaping their otherwise boring and pathetic lives. This is our time; we move in like the wind in the vents, unnoticed and part of the walls. We've got all we need to enter, grab and go. Gloved, hooded and in socks (on account of we kick off our shoes outside, just-in-case). No one sees or hears us. No way. We are way too good at this to ever get caught. Except when it looks like we might. We agree to run. Plain and simple. All we have is our backpacks so that makes it easy. I mean, we gotta eat.

Our targets are obvious enough; long left empty places with no signs of life. Empties, we call 'em. And it's best for all concerned that they stay that way. Dogs are the worst except they take 'em along if gone for a long time. And they usually don't clear out any of the food. Pay dirt for us. Dead of night when darkness consumes the land.

Sometimes a nosey neighbor will be up making tea or just being snoopy. We wait. They don't know we're watching. Usually that pesky stove light goes out soon enough. People are creatures of habit, don't you know it. And they don't notice nothin'. We can be just about anywhere and they just keep on talkin' and walkin'.

Our biggest hits are garages and those extra frigerators they keep fully stocked. We may even double back if we can't carry it all. The mother lode. Makes quick work to have it all handy and they usually have tons of cans out there like the end-of-the-world is comin' and damn it, they're going to live through it all out there in the garage. That I gotta see.

We're shadow people if there ever was any such thing. In fact, we see really good at night for some crazy reason and just sleep through those bright hours. That daytime stuff is just too much. Better for us too since we're kind of on the dirty side unless we sneak into a community park and slither in and out of the pool. We do pretty good most days. No one really cares about us anyways and since we're only there in a temporary way, we don't mind. Each band of misfits help each other out in big ways that matter. We can locate them in the cracks of the world. Yeah, it's noisy at times but we're so tired after running all over at night that it's our turn to sleep the sleep of the dead. And we do. Until we need to move on and show others the way. There are so many.

We get a few girls in the mix sometimes to do our scouting during the day. They don't mind the light so much and well, they kind of have a knack for finding out stuff that we can't. Like when someone goes on vacation. People love to blab about leaving town for their family vacation or summer house. The sisters look innocent so people talk to them. And they do okay with getting our food together too. It kind of bothers us that they're here without those soft things that only girls care about like kittens, baths and hot cocoa.

We work the towns in squares because that's how its all laid out and all. Plus we can point and no one gets lost. And we always set up these meet points in case we gotta run. Usually it's all good and we tumble back to our base with a whole mix of tins and bottles, all new like right off the supermarket shelf. There's a stir of activity when we return and the circle forms to count the goods. Everyone gets real quiet on account of remembering the sitting at tables and looking out with the warmth of the house and the feeling of home; what once was never to be again. The haul is the trigger. We see it every time. It only lasts a few minutes and feels like being in church sayin' a prayer which, I guess it is a sort of a blessing. Does God see all of this? We do this 'cuz he fell asleep on the job.

Sometimes we bump into an outlying shed or RV that pretty much is stocked except for those little fridges so we make light work. We can get into any place with a screwdriver and a pick. Locks are no big deal. Windows if the need arises. It's alarms that spook us out. Sometimes we hear a helicopter in the distance and run. It's not like their gonna see us from the sky but we know that we tripped something so we hightail it back into the shadows where we belong. And some neighborhoods have those rent-a-cops on patrol. They don't really care what's going on so we just wait until they pass.

I'm not sure how all this got started, me being the bandleader and all. Guess it got going a few years back after my parents split up and went their own ways. They figured I'd do okay being eighteen like that was all that was required to be indoors at night; a given. Found out pretty quick that my car was my bed until that got towed. Everything went to shit after that; too dirty to work and too many times late to bother. I went under-ground after meeting Billy, smoking behind the gas station of all places. He had long hair and painted his fingernails black. We became brothers pretty quick once our stories got air. He showed me all over that god-forsaken town until we decided to jump the night train to the next wide spot on the road and roll into the woods before the brakes hissed. We've been going that way ever since. It seemed a natural occurrence that our paths would cross. We were like twins that were separated at birth and were now, making up for lost time. It was Billy that introduced me to this nightlife of restocking the camps along the way. Since we didn't need money in any real way, this was enough. The demand for food would never end. He called me 'the Kid' and would laugh his roar of a laugh which got me laughing hard as well. I loved him and would follow him to the ends of the earth. Good a plan as any.

One day Billy came down with a fever that he never got over, at least the coughing part. We stayed put that winter and that may have been the real zinger. He got really skinny and we finally took him to one of those all night medical clinics where they kept him until an ambulance came and whisked him away to the local wherever. The last thing he said to me was, 'Keep 'em eating, Kid. Ok?' I nodded. That was that. I figure that one day, he'd get out and find me. He never did. The waiting was making me crazy so I just moved on to the next town, taking with me everything he taught me. I never heard his last name.

The thing of it is that there are more and more people showing up in the cracks. And most of them don't have their heads on right and may be shouting out or be real mean. They still need to eat. Somehow the food we take makes its way to them and is shared or traded or sold to others. Not sure how that works but I guess if you need money, there is a way. Might as well. I ran the game over and over with anyone who was up for it. Of course I needed help lugging the food from wherever it was unearthed. And then there was the distribution. There were always a few that were up for the score and got a real sense of power afterwards; spreading the bounty. I get it. I felt that way at first. Now, after many years, it seemed like more of a job and I was starting to think that there might be something else I could do that might yield something more lasting.

These thoughts starting taking over my life after I met Saint. She too had long hair and painted her fingernails black. She was a bit moody which I overlooked due mostly to her slight frame. After learning her turbulent upbringing, I could see why. She helped others by just being around. It wasn't so much anything she said for she didn't speak much. It was more a comforting aura she gave off. Maybe she just reminded others that they weren't alone. We all felt more human when she was around.

What she did for me was open a part of me that closed a long time ago except I didn't have a clue until she was crouching beside me one run. I almost didn't see her. I already knew I was alone since that first night in my car all those years ago. No, what she gave me was insight; into myself and a distant future. It surely was not going to be doing this. I mean, sure, I keep 'em fed and that's a good thing but I knew that there was a world out there with more. A lot more. A better version of myself.

Maybe I just got tired. I mean I'm twenty-five now and there isn't a city or town that I haven't seen or pilfered. And I got to thinking that maybe one of those would make sense. If so, I needed an exit. Nothing too obvious for sure. I was well-known now, at least in the cover of darkness. No, I had to hand off the riegns or at least make it appear that someone else took the lead and then disappear. It was then that I started to search for just the right person. It wasn't long before I found them.

As it turned out, Saint, of all people was a bit of a celebrity in her own right. She was good at getting people together with what (or who) they needed most. And it wasn't after a long conversation and a checklist. No sir. She just knew. So it didn't surprise that a few days later, a couple approached me; a guy and a girl that looked very much alike. Twins. Now there's a first. We huddled by the fire with small talk before my band for that night headed out. The couple tagged along and proved to be very good at following my unprovoked lead. They had the same moves and gestures. It was kind of creepy but equally forgetful which was a good recipe going forward. I decided that night that they would make excellent replacements so took them under my wing and taught them all I knew. We moved onto the next town under the blue moon. It was like being underwater. The whole landscape under this light like I've never seen before (or since). After catching the midnight train, I started thinking about my parents. So strange to be the offspring of two people that you never talk to anymore. I am an orphan now and have to make my own home. The tint of the night was mesmerizing. I fell under it's spell and got a whole lot older.

After we made the jump off, I was eager to leave right away and seek out my future. Above ground. We settled into the next crack easily and made the rounds for the grabs. The whole while I was distracted. It had officially run its course. I wanted more. It felt bad thinking it and I certainly wouldn't voice it in this group but the realization was there. This was my last run.

I woke early to the sunrise. A first. I had to slip out before anyone saw me. I emerged onto a road with only a truck stop on the far corner. Good enough. I needed to get cleaned up as best I could. I headed for the bathroom as fast as possible. All the shower stalls were full. I could hear singing.

The man in the mirror was my father. How strange I looked. My whole look was desperate; pale skin, greasy hair and like Saint, a slight frame. I simply hadn't noticed any of this before. Living in total darkness does have its advantages. Except now, I needed things. Clean things. The daylight was too honest. I had work to do if I was going to fit in. Humanity is a bitch, man.

As I emerged from the restroom hallway, I literally bumped into a lady. "Sorry" was all I could get out. "That's okay Honey. You hungry? I hate eating alone. C'mon. My treat." Her name was Shirley and she was just passing through. She looked like she could have been my aunt. I had trouble making eye contact. Everything felt so weird. The fork, the table and sitting on a padded bench. I felt like an alien.

She prattled on through the meal and finally noticed I hadn't said a word. "Honey, are you okay? You look like you could use a shower and some clean clothes. Leave it to me." Turns out she came through there enough to know the ropes. Before I could object, she had lead me to the men's side, commandeered a trucker's tokens and returned with some clothes. I got dressed and met up with her outside, squinting.

"Honey, you look brand new. How do you feel?" "OK. Thanks." "Can I give you a lift? I'm headed into the city." "Ok." was all I could say. Dry mouth. I liked Shirley just fine. Her voice filled the car and she passed me a twenty dollar bill before shooing me out and driving off with a wave.

I walked around and found some shade and a bench. All I could do was look around and try to make sense of it. I wasn't sure anymore about anything. It was really noisy. The energy was all wrong. My head in a vice, crushing. I can't remember who I was before the darkness. The light now was harsh and I felt cold, even in the sun. I was afraid. If I can't straighten all this out, the cracks will start pulling at me. I needed some help. I was lost in the daylight.

Just then, a car stopped at my feet and a familiar voice bellowed out in my direction. It was Shirley. She rolled down the window and yelled over, "Honey. I've been lookin' for you. C'mon over. Get in. We've got work to do. I'm gonna help you and you're gonna help me. OK? You're not alone anymore." I got in and started to cry.

Rae Whitney is a Fiction writer who appreciates any challenge she can find-especially if it involves writing. She now writes full time and has completed plays and short stories. Raised in Southern California, she has traveled the world, many times solo. She continues to explore, both near and far for story ideas and inspiration.

Her education includes a B.S. degree in Anthropology where her fascination with people and their languages began. She is fond of visiting new places whenever she can find the time. Her curious nature keeps her outdoors exploring nature, hiking and fleshing out her story ideas. She is currently editing her first book and resides in Ventura, CA.

When the bikers blow into town
Regi Claire

Throughout my teenage years I kept a black and white newspaper image pinned above my bed, of a blind metal woman with exposed viscera and snakes for hair: one of Giger's biomechanical creations. Now I live in another country far away, and I've become that woman. I walk my dog, smile, talk and masticate, I plait my hair, don the gear, log on, please or punish, transfer my funds – always mechanically. Sometimes I wonder if things will ever change. In the meantime we're out and about, Pitch and I, taking the air, sniffing and dawdling, not thinking too much.

It's a few minutes after midnight when the bikers blow into town. They ride along the main street in a cavalcade of throbbing engines. I am halfway down a side road, Pitch in tow, a dingy little street forever unblessed by the sun, lined with four-storey tenements and dark because the lights haven't been fixed in months. This is our second trek round the block, but she refuses to get down to business. 'Come on.' I give her a quick pat, then drag her away from under the hedge that, despite the ropes used to restrain it, encroaches on the pavement a little more every day.

We cross to the opposite side, towards an area choked with boards, shreds of plastic and foam insulation, and rubble spilling from heavy-duty garbage bags, an urban installation with its own drama. Several years ago the owner of the ground-floor apartment attempted to expand into the basement. He drove a mini-digger into his living room and started excavating, first inside, then outside, until the foundations developed cracks and the sewage pipes came loose. Eventually the man went bankrupt, then to pieces and had to be locked up 'for his own good'. As we amble past the safety fencing, I have to force myself not to loiter, have to disregard my sense of instant connection. I picture the latest graffiti on the door: 'illegal and dangerous building works'. No Banksie yet. A butterfly bush has taken root in the clots of earth that have been shoved back into the trench by the wall. There's a new owner now, I've heard, someone with plans to rebuild.

I trundle Pitch along the kerb with its flyblown litter, hoping the smells will set her off. A fine drizzle has begun to fall. It mists the air and muffles the rock music from the pub on the far corner. The bikes I heard earlier are parked outside, a staggered row of low-slung machines with Viking helmets on the saddles – no tails of pine martens or foxes dangling from the aerials, mercifully. Raindrops slide in runnels down the tanks and gleaming chromium. I let my fingers trace the curves of a Harley: still warm, smooth and damp as her skin would have been, then. And I know I can't go home now. It's October 14, another anniversary.

As soon as I pull Pitch through the door and into the noise, she ducks to wriggle out of her collar, then makes straight for the grimy murk under one of the banquettes near the emergency exit. I'll have to hose her off again afterwards, which will trigger the security lights in the garden and piss off the neighbours. But I'm up for it, tonight I am.

'What're you having?' someone shouts into my ear and I jerk away, almost colliding with a man in leather, tall, with a ponytail and a beer moustache.

The biker wipes the foam off his mouth, repeats, 'What're you having? I'm buying.'

'Oh, nothing, thanks. I've changed my mind.' I shake my head, hair flying, loose now that I'm off the clock. Whatever's made me say this? Some kind of last-chance redemption for sins yet to be committed? But I never change my mind. Shilly-shallying is for cowards – at least that's what I've been telling myself for the last five years.

And so I don't try to move past the man, and he doesn't need to step in my way. Instead he fishes a mobile from one of his fringed pockets and says, 'Aha, 00.21. I was born two minutes ago exactly.' He grins. 'Quarter of a century ago.'

'Too young for me.' I laugh, though I don't feel like it, a dry laugh, a little too high, and I stop before it can get out of control. 'Well, happy birthday,' I say, before signalling to the barmaid to order their house vodka flavoured with honey and chilli pepper.

The biker mumbles something and flips a twenty on the counter, next to Pitch's lead and collar. 'This is on me, I insist,' he says. Then he gives me a sidelong look and adds quietly, 'God, I am sorry. All that prattle about birthdays. You've lost your dog, haven't you?'

I pause long enough for him to squirm, which isn't easy in sweaty leathers, and don't I know it. No, Pitch is not the leaving kind, I tell him, unlike some people. I turn my face away, make it hard and defiant like the carved figurehead at the prow of a ship. When I glance over to where Pitch lies hidden in the shadows, I glimpse for a moment not the shape of my dog but a stillness that crouches, so pale and forlorn, so out of reach that I have to close my eyes.

The biker says the usual things like what a lovely accent, where am I from, and oh he has never been but it's on his bucket list, and what's made me choose this cold, damn country, am I alone here, and so on and so forth until my vodka arrives. Then my second vodka arrives. I've just had a couple of sips, less numbing, sweeter and friendlier despite the extra lemon and that killer kick of chilli, when Queen come on and the regulars start to thump their table. Something shatters on the floor and I see Pitch scramble towards the spillage. Unlike me, she never runs from danger. By the time I've pushed past the drinkers roaring, 'We will, we will rock you', Pitch is licking at a puddle of shards that reek of whisky, and she is limping. Everyone seems to watch as I try to haul her away. My top keeps slipping, revealing my G-string version of a bra. Then Birthday Boy picks her up.

There's a triangle of glass lodged in one of her front paws. I ease it out, put it on a nearby table, the regulars', then tug a paper napkin from under a slopping tumbler to press against the wound. She barely winces.

'Bitch!' I say, just as the track finishes. 'Oh, Bitch!' When I'm upset, I always forget to pronounce properly.

People turn to stare. That's when one of the regulars rises to his feet, a big unshaven guy with a flare of veins across his face, and I realise it must be his tumbler I've interfered with. 'What was that?' he says before I can apologise, and he sounds so pretend-calm I feel myself shrink. 'Where the fuck have you sprung from?' His fist shoots out and he tosses something at me. I catch it instinctively.

I am seated in a chair at the short end of the L-shaped bar, my vodka on the polished counter in front of me, at chin height. My right hand is wrapped in a dark scarf with a red paisley pattern of skulls. I feel confused in a time-lag sort of way. What's happened? The Jukebox is going; the answer, I'm told, is blowing in the wind. The voices of the regulars over by the window ebb and swell like waves in the aftermath of a storm. I unwind the scarf. My palm is smeared with blood, and it's sore. My left hand is marked too,though not as much. When I check my knuckles I find them unblemished – no abrasions, nothing. But then, why should there be? I haven't been struggling to hold on to anything, struggling to keep my grip.

The barmaid leans over the counter. 'It's not as bad as it looks,' she says, squinting down between clumped mascara lashes. 'A couple of nicks is all. I doused them with our best gin, Pickering's Navy Strength, and you passed out. When you get home, tape it up with some gauze.' She gives me a big smile. 'You'll live.'

She has no idea what she's just said.

How do you know? I want to ask. Instead I say, 'Where's my dog?' I don't add, Bitch, pronounced deliberately this time.

She seems surprised. 'That biker with the ponytail took her away. Said he'd told you. They've left.'

'Birthday Boy?' I survey the bar. No bikers.

'Actually, he said it was your birthday. Said he'd go back to yours. Is he your birthday present? A biker Strip-O-Gram?' She smiles again, puckering her lips.

My birthday?

No sign of any motorbikes outside, so I hurry through the empty streets, through the rain that's coming down in sheets now. It must be well after one.

Past the building site where someone has dumped a battered old suitcase and a bathtub. How could they have – and in the middle of the night? From a wall grating I catch a glimmer of something, like a candle being snuffed out. Though that too is impossible. No one lives there. It's all closed off, and the earth has been filled in, hasn't it? The hedge bulges even more over the pavement, probably due to the rain that's been filtering down through the thick black soil, swelling the roots, and the worms.

The lights of an ambulance streak past the shop windows on the main street, across the wet asphalt and water-filled potholes, their reflections like silent screams come briefly back to life. One, two, three, four... If screams can be silent, do they have an echo? Do they echo within themselves? Echo and echo until they cause ripples all around, in the water, the air, the earth, in fire? I believe they do. Because I can hear them now, even with my hands over my ears.

When I reach my apartment building, there is no Pitch, no Birthday Boy, no bike. Where are they? Pitch! I want to cry. Pitch! Pitch! But that would rouse the whole street, with everyone yelling at me to shut the fuck up.

After three more circuits of the neighbourhood I allow myself to give up. If only I could remember what I said to that biker. Did I tell him where I live? What I do for a living? I remain standing at the front door, rain dripping off my hair, my cheeks, my chin, getting soaked to the bone. Through a gap between the buildings opposite I see a night bus lumber past, a home on wheels crammed with laughing, farting, snoring life. And then I let it all go. Centre myself, locate the safe place inside the dereliction that is me.

The police don't seem to take my call seriously. 'Get back in touch if your dog hasn't turned up within the next 24 hours. Someone's probably given him shelter. '

'Her,' I can't help correcting. The officer exhales noisily. 'Him, her, whatever,' he says, sleepy-bored. 'You have our number. Goodnight.' He hangs up.

Afterwards I get the emergency bottle of spirits from the fridge, pour half over my palms and drink the rest neat.

I dream of a submarine base hewn out of rock and a woman singing in its twilit cavern, her voice rising and falling amidst the lapping of the sea; I dream of her laughter and mine, of the sound of our paddles, hers up ahead already widening the distance between us until it becomes unbridgeable, though she doesn't know it and nor do I, yet; I dream of the slap of the waves urging us on, of the sudden scream of the wind as she rounds the headland first, into what should have been the day's crowning glory: the sun sinking red-gold into western waters, against the outline of a little island advertised for family holidays – where she will be found the following morning, drifting in her yellow safety vest.

My hair is still damp when I wake up, tangled in a blanket. As soon as I open my eyes I know things aren't right. No Pitch to greet me. No duvet. The lights are on. The smell of smoke. Then I remember and I start weeping. The door creaks and a man comes in. Hair down to his shoulders, leather trousers, boots, no shirt, a cigarette pinched between his lips. I try to make myself small. Tiny small. Like a ball of fur or feathers that can roll and slip through fingers, burrow down deep or fly away... But of course I can't do either. So I try not think. Try not to recall the vile, drunken things I said when he rang the bell and demanded to be let in.

These days whenever I'm in a situation that threatens to get out of hand, I tell myself that if death isn't at stake, it's all right to watch. So I watch. Watch myself in this instance. Mechanically and with mild interest, the way I've learnt to survive. I believe we should all be condemned to fight for our lives at one point or another. If we perish, well, we perish. We won't be the first, nor the last. I picture the metal woman in the black and white newspaper clipping above the bed of my teenage self, and I'm as ready as I'll ever be. I can guess what will happen next.

Three summers ago a neighbour chopped down the rosebush in our garden, perhaps because she felt her bedroom invaded by its drowsy, wine-red fragrance. The following year the plant grew back stronger and thornier, its roots proliferating inside the earth, spreading all along that side of the house, its flower sunscented now and colourless, the purest white.

'How is it,' I ask the biker, 'that the suffering never stops?'

'What suffering?' he says and shrugs. Then he stubs the cigarette out on the heel of his boot and, with one last glance at me, walks off towards the door. 'By the way, your Pitch-Bitch is in the kitchen, tanked up to the eyeballs.'

And all the while I'd been waiting for him to get started so I could fight back. Fight him. Bite him. Scratch him. Whatever it takes. But he just stood there, blowing smoke, looking. Not lifting even his little finger.

And now? Andnowandnowandnowand–?

I can stop him yet. I can hear his footsteps going down the stairs. Will I call him back – before he returns to being a biker with a ponytail, dressed in the skin of animals? Will I?

Regi Claire is a novelist and short story writer twice shortlisted for a Saltire Scottish Book of the Year award and longlisted for MIND Book of the Year and the Edge Hill Prize for best collection. Born and raised in Switzerland, she has been based in Scotland for many years. She is an exophonic author (her mother tongue is Swiss German).Her work has appeared in Ambit, Best British Short Stories, Edinburgh Review, Litro Magazine, Litro Online, New Writing Scotland, Tears in the Fence and many other publications worldwide, also in translation.

EYELANDS INTERNATIONAL SHORT STORY CONTEST

Eyelands.gr *literary magazine in collaboration with Strange Days Books organize an annual international short story competition, which is the only international short story contest based in Greece. Every year, writers from all the continents of the world participate in it. The competition consists of two categories; Greek an International (for the international section we only accept stories in English).*

The competition has been running continuously for the past seven years, offering hundreds of writers the opportunity to see their short story printed in one of our collections, created through the contest entries. For many of these writers it is the first time that a story of theirs is printed in a book or featured online. The English section of the competition has been recognized as a truly reliable, fair and serious short story competition. Every year, many reputable websites, post the announcement of our contest, which has earned its reputation year after year, by honoring all its promises, following the rules meticulously and meeting all criteria that allow a contest to gain respect and recognition on an international level.

EYELANDS BOOK AWARDS

In 2018 *we decided to launch a new contest, Eyelands Book Awards, an international contest that gives the opportunity to a writer to win a great prize; a holiday in Athens, Greece, where he/she will have the chance to talk about his/her work to Greek readers and meet Greek writers in a special ceremony. This is the grand prize for writers who have already published their book. But there's more. Eyelands Book Awards also gives the opportunity to an unpublished writer to win a contract and see her/his book published from Strange Days Books. There are also prizes for the winners of the three different categories, as well as nominations of five writers per category. Join us next year! Send us your submission and win the grand prize, visit Athens or see your book published!*

For more info please visit our website https://eyelandsawards.com

STRANGE DAYS BOOKS

Editions in English

2013/ 52 eyelands, a sentimental guide through the Greek islands
by Gregory Papadoyiannis
2013/ Slowly but thoroughly
by Ben D. Fischer
2014 / The Time collection
Eyelands 4th ISSC /The short listed stories
2015 / Borderline stories
Eyelands 5th ISSC /The short listed stories
2016 / Stories in colour
Eyelands 6th ISSC /The short listed stories
2017 /Strange Love Affairs
Eyelands 7th ISSC /The short listed stories
2018 / Dreams
Eyelands 1st flash fiction contest /The short listed stories
201 /Luggage
Eyelands 8th ISSC /The short listed stories
2019/ Spring
Eyelands 2st flash fiction contest /The short listed stories

Strange Days Books
Social Cooperative Publishing House
Address: Chimarras 6, Rethymno, 74100, Crete, Greece
tel:+2831503835
email: strangedaysbooks@gmail.com
www.facebook.com/STRANGEDAYSBOOKS
Copyright© Strange Days Books
Cover design: © *strangeland*

ISBN: 9781700174369

Printed in Great Britain
by Amazon

23848775R10067